"Grab that branch, Elizabeth," Thad instructed in a voice that reminded her of far-off and friendly thunder.

"Oh!" She was about to place her foot on the stepladder when she heard the sound of ripping cloth.

"What was that?" Thad asked.

Elizabeth's cheeks flamed as she tried to unsnag her lacy petticoat from the branch.

"Here, I'd better do that," Thad told her.

She held on for dear life while he flipped back her skirt and buried his hands in yards of linen and lace looking for the hangup. It seemed to take forever for him to find it.

"There," he said finally. "Now put your arms on my shoulders and I'll help you down."

She'd never been this close to him before. Never close enough to see that his eyes were very blue. Never close enough to smell his cologne, which made her think of saddles and sex. And seeing his fingers rubbing the torn piece of lace between them made her mouth go dry . . .

WHAT ARE *LOVESWEPT* ROMANCES?

They are stories of true romance and touching emotion. We believe those two very important ingredients are constants in our highly sensual and very believable stories in the *LOVESWEPT* line. Our goal is to give you, the reader, stories of consistently high quality that may sometimes make you laugh, sometimes make you cry, but are always fresh and creative and contain many delightful surprises within their pages.

Most romance fans read an enormous number of books. Those they truly love, they keep. Others may be traded with friends and soon forgotten. We hope that each *LOVESWEPT* romance will be a treasure—a "keeper." We will always try to publish

LOVE STORIES YOU'LL NEVER FORGET
BY AUTHORS YOU'LL ALWAYS REMEMBER

The Editors

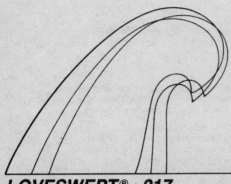

LOVESWEPT® • 217

Sandra Brown
Fanta C

 BANTAM BOOKS
TORONTO • NEW YORK • LONDON • SYDNEY • AUCKLAND

FANTA C

A Bantam Book / November 1987

If you would be interested in receiving protective vinyl
covers for your Loveswept books, please write to this address
for information:

Loveswept
Bantam Books
P.O. Box 985
Hicksville, NY 11802

ISBN 0-553-21836-0

Published simultaneously in the United States and Canada

PRINTED IN THE UNITED STATES OF AMERICA

O   0 9 8 7 6 5 4 3 2 1

One

The first time was enchanted.

We made love in the stable amid the smell of hay and horses and dust. Our coupling was hot and lusty. Our bodies were shiny with sweat when it was over. Replete, we lay with limbs entwined. Straw was tangled in my hair. He playfully plucked out pieces of it, while I delighted in the way the sun shone in through the cracks in the walls, casting stripes of light and shadow on his wide hairy chest.

It had been destined to happen, though the selection of the time had been exclusively his. Mounted on one of my father's prized Thoroughbreds, I had returned to the stable after my daily ride. My heart had begun to beat vigorously at the sight of the stable foreman leaning against the corner of the building. No one else was in the yard.

I looked at him with the haughty condescension passed down to me through generations of aristocratic breeding. He, in no great hurry, sauntered *forward. Smiling arrogantly, he raised his hands and placed them around my waist to assist me off the sidesaddle. Wanting to shake his unshakable self-confidence and conceit, I deliberately let my body slide enticingly down the front of his before my booted feet touched the ground. I watched his eyes grow dark, but my triumph was short-lived.*

Defying convention and propriety, he continued to hold me close against him. I gazed up at him with unmitigated desire. It was made even stronger because he was employed by my father and far beneath my social status. Any kind of intimate relationship between the stable foreman and me was forbidden. Deliciously, temptingly so.

Then, too, he was Irish. I, English. He was wild and undisciplined and possessed of a temperament as stormy as the Irish Sea. I had been reared in an atmosphere of gentility and refinement. I knew French and Latin. He had only a rudimentary knowledge of English and was frequently overheard using vulgarities the meanings of which I could not begin to guess. If the gossip was true, in his possession a bottle of whisky rarely outlived the night. I was sometimes allowed to sip one glass of sherry before dinner, and then only on special occasions. My hands were immaculate. His were not. But that didn't matter when he slid them around my waist and pulled me closer still.

He bent his head and kissed me as though it were his right instead of tantamount to the capital offense it would be should we be discovered. A lock of his long, unruly hair brushed across my smooth brow as he dipped his head lower and pressed his open mouth upon mine.

Though he was responding to the desire he had no doubt seen in my eyes, his audacity enraged me. I pushed against the front of his leather jerkin. But I was fighting a losing battle, not only against his superior strength, but with myself and the passionate stirring of my blood. Admittedly, I didn't try too hard to escape his embrace or his marauding tongue when it thrust between my lips and deflowered my mouth.

At that point, I felt quite faint.

Breathless and weak, I stumbled along behind him as he drew me into the deep, musty shadows of Father's stable. This is what I had wanted, wasn't it? Isn't this what all those smoldering looks that we had been exchanging for weeks should culminate in? Hadn't I, with accidental touches and provocative postures, issued an invitation for him to do just this? Secrets were about to be revealed to me. Didn't I crave to know what the servant girls whispered about behind their hands?

Even had I changed my mind, he wouldn't have allowed it. He pressed me against the slats of one of the stalls. The hay was knee-deep, sweet-smelling, and fresh. It was warm inside the building. And dim. Dust motes waltzed in the air as crazily as my senses were spinning. With his lips still glued to mine, he angled his body forward so that I might feel the evidence of his desire behind his tight britches. The strong, agile body I had safely admired from behind the curtains in my bedroom window now pressed against me with alarming familiarity. My thighs trembled, but parted obediently as he wedged his knees between them and rammed his hips up and forward.

His hands went straight for the stock tied in a demure bow around my throat. He undid the knot with a gentle jerk and began unwinding the white silk, dropping it into the hay when it came off. The pearl buttons of my blouse were no deterrent to his questing hands. They slipped from their hand-embroidered holes without protest.

I gasped when I felt his work-rough hands on my breasts. My batiste camisole made him impatient. He shoved it down and my breasts fell free into his callused palms.

Overwhelmed with the strange sensations coursing through me, my eyelids fluttered closed. My head fell back against the slats, and I surrendered totally, when his mouth descended to cover my quivering flesh with ardent kisses. I had never imagined that a man's lips and teeth and tongue were capable of giving such incredible pleasure. It was sinful, wasn't it? Didn't The Book of Common Prayer describe these feelings rivering through me as carnal delights? They were so terribly wicked. Yet so splendid. My nipples became hard and pointed beneath the damp, rapid stroking of his tongue. Arching my back, I pushed them deeper into his mouth. Involuntarily, I cried out his name.

"Shh, shh, my love," he whispered in the lilting, melodic accent I loved. "It's careful we must be."

His hands exercised no decorum. They obeyed no rules. They slipped beneath the skirt of my ruby velvet riding habit, tangled in the layers of lacy petticoats, and waded their way through my clothing until they touched my naked skin. Roughly whispered endearments, enriched with his decidedly Irish flamboyance, filled my ears as he fondled me intimately with a tenderness at odds with his growing impatience.

He opened his trousers and I saw him. The extent of his arousal frightened me. He saw my fear and soothed it with words of comfort and reassurance. His manhood was warm and smooth and *hard as he entered me, stretching me, filling me. Our moans filtered through the shadows of the stable. The exquisite pleasure of our joined bodies lifted me out of myself. I plowed furrows through his hair with my fingers. He kissed my breasts fervently. With each thrust he delved deeper into me. And deeper still. Until—*

"Elizabeth!"

Elizabeth Burke was rudely yanked out of her fantasy by her sister's exasperated voice. Eyes which had been cornily described as china-blue blinked into focus the woman standing on the threshold of her gift shop. Her sister's face was drawn into a frown as affectionate and tolerant as it was disapproving. Lilah, younger by two years than Elizabeth, shook her head and clicked her tongue. "You're at it again, I see."

"At what?"

"Don't play dumb with me, Elizabeth." She shook her index finger at her sister. "You were daydreaming. At least a million miles away."

"I was not. I was, uh, thinking about the order I'm filling out." Elizabeth rearranged a stack of papers on the glass showcase to give her lie credibility. Her cheeks were as warm with embarrassment over having been caught fantasizing as they were flushed from the heat of the fantasy itself. As she feared, her preceptive sister wasn't fooled.

"You're blushing. If it was that good, share it with me." Lilah dropped down onto one of the high, velvet-cushioned stools Elizabeth had provided for her customers to use while looking at the merchandise in the shop. The stool had a lacy white wrought-iron back. Lilah stacked her hands on the crest of it and gazed up at her sister. "Give. I'm all ears."

"You're all baloney. I wasn't fantasizing about anything except the ringing of the cash register. What do you think of these perfume bottles? They're made in West Germany." She pushed the catalogue across the countertop.

Lilah gave the glossy pictures a cursory glance. "Very nice."

"Nice *and* expensive. Do you think a high-ticket item like that will sell?"

"It depends on how unfaithful the buyer has been."

Lilah had a jaundiced attitude toward matrimony, even for this day and age. Elizabeth didn't agree. "Not every man who shops here is buying a present for his wife to ease a guilty conscience."

"Of course not. Some of them are shopping for their mistresses," Lilah said drolly. "Just look at them."

She waved toward the paned-glass bay window through which the elegant lobby of the Hotel Cavanaugh could be seen. It was crawling with people, mostly men, who were either waiting to check out or check in. With few exceptions they were traveling businessmen who were uniformly dressed in varying shades of dark wool worsted. Most carried leather attaché cases and trenchcoats. They all seemed to be under a deadline and wore similar anxiety-ridden expressions.

"Hurrying home to the little woman after a week of high living on the road," Lilah said disdainfully. She was a feminist. In her older sister's opinion Lilah carried her battle for equality of the sexes a bit too far. "I'm convinced that at least half of them have dallied while they were away from home and hearth. Aren't you lucky that their guilt is good for your business?"

"What a wretched thing to say. Just because you've elected not to marry doesn't mean that there aren't happy marriages."

"Maybe one in a million."

"I believe that my customers come in here to buy gifts for the wives they have missed and will be very glad to return home to."

"You also believe in the tooth fairy. Get your head out of the clouds." Teasingly Lilah reached up and tugged on a strand of Elizabeth's pale blond hair. "Join the real world."

"You don't make the real world sound like a very pleasant place to be." Elizabeth swatted aside Lilah's hand and rubbed at a smudge on the glass showcase.

"That's because I'm not viewing it through rose-colored glasses."

"What's wrong with a little romance?"

"Nothing! I'm down on love, marriage, and all that stuff. I never said anything derogatory about *sex*."

Elizabeth recoiled. "Neither did I. And keep your voice down. Somebody might hear you."

"So what if they do? You're the only one not talking about sex these days. Aren't you getting lonesome?" She ignored Elizabeth's sour look. "Sex, sex, sex. There, see? I didn't get struck by lightning. I wasn't swallowed by a whale. I didn't turn into a pillar of salt. I'm still here."

"Well, I wish you'd go away," Elizabeth grumbled. She knew what was coming. No matter how their conversations started, they always ended with a discussion about her love life . . . or lack of one.

The differences in their personalities and philosophies were reflected in their appearances. They bore a striking resemblance to each other. Both were blond, but Elizabeth's hair was finer and straighter than her sister's. Her features were delicately drawn. Lilah's were more voluptuous. Both had blue eyes, but Elizabeth's were as serene as a country pond while Lilah's were as restless as the north Atlantic.

Elizabeth would have felt comfortable dressing out of a Victorian lady's armoire. Lilah went for the most avant-garde fashions. Elizabeth was cautious and studious. She carefully weighed the potential consequences before taking the first step onto unfamiliar ground. Lilah had always been the impetuous, aggressive one. That was why she felt free to be so outspoken about her sister's personal life.

"As long as you're working in so fertile a playground, why don't you get in on the game?"

Elizabeth pretended not to understand. "Don't you have a session this afternoon?" Lilah was a physical therapist.

"Not till four-thirty and stop changing the subject. When one of these men catches your eye," she said, waving toward the twin bay windows on either side of the shop's door, "grab him. What have you got to lose?"

"My self-respect for one thing," Elizabeth said crisply. "I'm not like you, Lilah. To me sex isn't a game, as you call it. It's love. It involves a commitment." Lilah rolled her eyes as though saying "Here comes the sermon." "You've never been in love so how could you know?"

Lilah stopped clowning. "Okay, look, I know you loved John. It was storybook all the way. College sweetheart. One soda, two straws. Your love affair with him was so damn sweet it was sickening. But he's dead, Lizzie."

When she called her sister by the pet name, they were getting to the heart of the matter. She reached across the counter and took Elizabeth's hand, pressing it between her own. "He's been dead for two years. You weren't cut out to be a nun. Why are you living like one?"

"I'm not. I've got this shop. You know how much time it takes. It's not as though I'm sitting at home, pining away and feeling sorry for myself. I'm out every day earning a living for the children and me. I'm involved in their activities."

"And what about *your* activities? When you're not working and the kids are bedded down for the night, then what? What does the Widow Burke do for herself?"

"The Widow Burke is too tired by that time to do anything other than go to bed."

"Alone." Elizabeth released a long-suffering sigh that was indicative of how tired she was of this perpetual argument. Lilah paid no attention to it. "How long are you going to settle for fantasies?"

"I don't fantasize."

Lilah laughed. "I know better. You're a hopeless romantic. For as long as I can remember, you were tying tea towels on my head and making me a lady-in-waiting to you, the princess, who was waiting for Prince Charming."

"And then when he arrived, you threw him into a pit with a fire-breathing dragon," Elizabeth said, laughing at the childhood recollection, "and made him fight to prove his worth."

"Yeah, but when the dragon got to be too much for the prince, I'd run in and rescue him."

"That's the difference between us. I was always confident that Prince Charming would slay the dragon without any trouble."

"Are you waiting for another prince, Lizzie? I hate to break the news to you, but they just don't exist."

"I know they don't," she said wistfully.

"So settle for something less. Like an ordinary guy who puts on his pants one leg at a time. And takes them off the same way," Lilah added with a mischievous grin.

Elizabeth slipped back into her fantasy. The stable hand hadn't taken off his pants at all. He'd been too impatient. Impatience like that was exciting. Her heart fluttered, bringing her back into the present. This erotic daydreaming must stop. It was ridiculous. She blamed her absorption with sex on her sister. If Lilah wouldn't talk about it all the time, then maybe she wouldn't be reminded how deprived she was.

"Well, even the ordinary men are hard to find," she said. "And I'm not going to tackle one as he walks past this door."

"Okay then, let's focus on someone closer to home." Lilah's brows furrowed. "What about your neighbor?"

Elizabeth got busy with a squirt bottle of Windex and a cleaning cloth. "What neighbor?"

"How many single men live in the house behind you, Elizabeth?" Lilah asked with asperity. "The hunky one with gray hair. Broad shoulders."

Elizabeth scrubbed harder at the smudge on the glass. "Mr. Randolph?"

Lilah's laugh was downright wicked. "Mr. Randolph?" she mimicked in a high, singsong voice. "Don't play innocent with me. You've noticed him, right?"

Elizabeth stashed the bottle of glass cleaner and the cloth behind the counter and, with annoyance, pushed back a wayward strand of hair. "He's the only single man in my neighborhood."

"So why don't you invite him over for dinner some evening?"

"Why don't you mind your own business?"

"Or wear something absolutely scandalous the next time you mow the grass. Sunbathe topless."

"Lilah, really! Besides, summer's over. It's too cold to sunbathe."

Lilah winked licentiously. "That'll make your nipples hard."

"I'm not listening to this."

"If that's too much, then do something traditional. Ask him to repair your toaster."

"It's not broken."

"So break it!" Lilah came off the stool and faced her sister with obvious aggravation. "At a time when he's bound to see you, look a little helpless and distraught."

"You wouldn't."

"Hell no, *I* wouldn't. But, as we've already established, I'm not you. I was never the damsel in distress in those fantasies you dreamed up."

By an act of will, Elizabeth got a grip on her temper. "It's odd that you poke fun at my fantasies. Wasn't it your idea for me to name my shop Fantasy?"

"I don't poke fun at your fantasies. They're as much a part of you as your fingerprints. Would I have given you that car tag if I didn't think it fit your character?"

The car tag Lilah had given her last Christmas read FANTA C. She had been appalled at the gag gift, but Lilah had had it registered with the state bureau. Without going through miles of red tape and all the rigmarole of having it changed, she was stuck with it for at least a year.

"That license plate is a constant source of embarrassment to me," she told her sister now. "Every time someone pulls up beside me, I can tell he's wondering what's going on inside my dirty mind."

Lilah laughed. "Good. Why don't you roll down the window and tell him? Or better yet, act it out."

Lilah's laughter was infectious. Before she realized it, Elizabeth was laughing with her. "You're incorrigible."

"Yes I am," Lilah admitted without a shred of remorse.

"And I know you have my best interest at heart."

"I do. You'll be thirty soon. I don't want you to wake up ten years from now and still be alone. Your kids won't even be around by then. You could get committed waiting to get committed. Prince Charming is not going to come beating down your door, Lizzie. He won't step out of your fantasies and take you in his arms. You might have to seize the initiative."

Elizabeth, knowing that her sister was unfortunately right, looked away. As she did, she spied the morning newspaper she hadn't gotten around to reading yet. "Maybe I'll set my cap for him." She pointed down at the picture of the man on the front page.

"Adam Cavanaugh," Lilah read. "Owner of the chain, I suppose?"

"Yes. He's going to be here this week on an inspection tour. The hotel management and all the lessees have been put on the alert."

"He's good-looking," Lilah remarked matter-of-factly. "But face it, he's superrich, superhandsome, and more than likely a superjerk. An international playboy. He's still a fantasy character, Lizzie. If I were you, , I'd look for a bedmate who's a little more accessible."

Elizabeth made a face at her. "Before you run off all my customers with your filthy language, will you please get out of here?"

"I was going anyway," Lilah said loftily. "If I don't, I'll be late for my four-thirty appointment. Toodle-doo." She waggled her fingers airily as she sailed out, slipping between the two men who sidestepped for her. Lilah winked at both of them. They paused to watch her retreating form appreciatively before they entered Fantasy.

One had Elizabeth gift wrap a slender silver bracelet for "my wife," he said. Elizabeth wondered, then chided herself for letting Lilah rouse her suspicions.

The second man took more time deliberating before buying a basket of chocolates wrapped in pink cellophane and tied with a pink bow and silk orchid. As she rang up the sale Elizabeth assessed his merits. Nice chin. Nice hands. But he parted his hair funny. The sleeves of his jacket were a trifle too long. The seat of his trousers was baggy.

Good Lord, she thought as the man left the shop with his purchase. Was she actually beginning to listen to Lilah? Heaven forbid that she ever take her sister's advice.

On an evening when she most wanted peace and quiet, she should have known that it would be too much to ask for. When she arrived home, she found chaos.

Her eight-year-old daughter, Megan, and six-year-old son, Matt, were in the backyard with their babysitter, Mrs. Alder. All three were nearly hysterical. Elizabeth cut the motor of her car, pushed open the door, and hit the ground running, certain that the house must be on fire.

"What is it? What's going on? Is someone hurt?"

"Baby!" Megan wailed. "She's in the tree."

"We called her and called her, but she can't get down."

"She's stuck up there and it's getting dark."

"Get her down, Mom. Please."

"I couldn't, Mrs. Burke, or I would have," a breathless Mrs. Alder said above the children's crying voices.

Elizabeth, thinking that something dreadful had happened, was relieved to learn that the tumult was over nothing more than the new kitten. The cat was stranded in the sycamore tree, all right, but no one was choking, or bleeding, or had a broken bone, or any of the other disasters that their weeping and wailing had warranted.

"All right, everybody calm down," she shouted. When the crying subsided to a few juicy sobs, she said, "You're raising a big ruckus over nothing."

"But she's just a baby kitten."

"And she's scared. Listen to her crying." Matt's lower lip began to wobble again.

"We'll get Baby down and well before dark," Elizabeth said. "Mrs. Alder, if you'd—"

"I'd like to help you, Mrs. Burke, but if I don't leave right away I'll be late for my evening job and I've got to stop at home first."

"Oh." Elizabeth glanced up at the stranded kitten, which was mewing pitiably. "You'd better get going then, Mrs. Alder. I'll take it from here."

"I'd sure help you if I could. I hate to leave you, knowing that— "

"I understand. Don't worry about it. I'll see you tomorrow."

The babysitter left. Elizabeth watched her go with regret. A helping hand wouldn't have hurt, even if it was the hand of an elderly lady.

Widowhood had its psychological and social detriments, but sometimes not having a man around the house was simply a pain. At times like this she got angry with John for getting killed and leaving her alone with all the responsibilities that come with having a family.

But, as in similar situations, Elizabeth gritted her teeth and approached the problem pragmatically and with a "what choice do I have?" spirit of determination. It was apparent that the damn cat wasn't going to fly out of the tree on command like a pet canary.

She and her children stood beneath the tree, analyzing the problem.

"How are you going to get up there, Mom?"

"I don't think she can," Matt said dismally in response to his sister's worried question.

"Of course I can." Elizabeth gave them a falsely confident smile. "Lilah and I used to climb trees all the time."

"Aunt Lilah said you were always a 'fraidy cat.' "

"Well, I'm not. And I wasn't. And that just shows how much Aunt Lilah knows." Elizabeth had an ax to grind with her sister the next time she saw her.

"Maybe we should call the fire apartment," Matt suggested.

"*De*partment, stupid," Megan corrected him.

For once Elizabeth let Megan's slur pass and said sharply, "Matthew, bring me the stepladder from the garage." She didn't want her children to think she was a coward. The boy ran to do her bidding. "I'd better change before—"

"Oh, Mom, please don't," Megan said, catching her mother's sleeve as she headed for the house. "Just seeing you has already calmed Baby down. If you go inside she might start crying again and I can't stand it. I really can't." Cloudy tears welled up in Megan's eyes. Elizabeth couldn't resist their appeal. Besides, just then Matt came huffing up carrying the stepladder.

"It's not tall enough, Mom."

"It'll have to do." She dusted her hands. "Well, here I go." She placed the ladder beneath the tree. Stepping out of her pumps, she climbed to the top platform of the ladder, which only put her a few feet above the ground. By stretching on tiptoe, she was able to grasp the lowest branch. She hung by it, suspended for a moment, before walking up the stout trunk of the tree until she could get a foot into the lowest notch.

Matt jumped up and down and clapped his hands. "Gee, Mom, you're just like Rambo."

"Thanks," Elizabeth said grimly. The palms of her hands were already scraped raw. The mean part about it was that Lilah probably could have shinned up the tree and already been safely down by now with the kitten in her arms. As it was, the kitten was still stranded and Elizabeth still had a long way to go.

"I can see your petticoat," Megan observed.

"Sorry, but I can't help that." Elizabeth puffed as she struggled to heave herself up onto the branch. Finally she succeeded and paused to rest. The cat had started to whine again.

"Hurry, Mom."

"I'm hurrying," she said testily. She worked her way up through the branches of the tree, careful never to look down. Heights made her dizzy.

At last she reached the kitten. Speaking to it soothingly, she cupped the animal's belly in her hand and lifted it off its perch. Making her way down was a considerably greater challenge, working with only one hand. She made it to the halfway mark without mishap and called down to the children. "I'm going to drop her from here. You'll have to catch her, Megan. Ready?"

"Are you sure?"

"I'm sure. Ready?"

"Ready," Megan said dubiously.

Feeling like the most heartless creature ever born and ignoring her childrens' reproachful eyes, Elizabeth let go of the kitten. With all four legs extended, the cat landed on the ground at Megan's feet.

The girl reached for the kitten, but it was terrified and bolted. It raced across the grassy yard, through the hedge, and straight between Thad Randolph's feet. Screaming, the children raced after Baby, unmindful of their mother's anguished pleas for them to stay where they were.

She rested her cheek against the trunk of the tree and resigned herself to playing out this farce to its very end. She listened as her children explained to the single man who lived in the house behind them what had happened. Their young voices rang through the late afternoon tranquilly.

Periodically, Elizabeth could hear Mr. Randolph making a comment like "You don't say?" "I'm sure Baby *was* frightened." "No, of course it wasn't your fault, Matt. Kittens just naturally like to climb trees."

"And now our mom is stuck up there."

Elizabeth groaned and squeezed her eyes shut. She had been praying that they'd tell their tale and that he'd eventually tire of it. She envisioned him patting them on their heads dismissively and carrying into his house the sack of groceries he'd been holding in his arms when the cat charged between his feet.

But when Elizabeth opened her eyes, she saw through the branches of the sycamore that the sack of groceries was sitting on the hood of his Jeep

Cherokee wagon and that he was holding the kitten in his large hands. Baby was curled into a ball and obviously enjoying his attention.

"Your mother got the kitten down?"

"Uh-huh. But she's still up in the tree. Mo-o-o-o-om!" Matt yodeled across the yard.

"I don't think she can get down."

Elizabeth had always been proud of Megan's intuition, which was advanced far beyond her years. Now she wanted to throttle her for it.

"I'm . . . I'm fine," Elizabeth called out. She hastily placed her stockinged foot on the next branch and lowered herself to it. Lilah had advised her to appear helpless and distraught in front of her bachelor neighbor, but this was ridiculous.

She saw Thad Randolph pass the purring kitten to Megan, but he was distracted. He was looking at the tree with narrowed eyelids as though trying to spot her through the branches. The trio, with Baby nestled secure in Megan's arms, came walking across the adjoining lawns.

"She's just a mom," Matt said disparagingly. "I don't think she can climb trees good."

"You said she was just like Rambo," Megan said in her mother's defense.

"She got up there, but I don't think she can get down." Matt looked up at Thad solemnly. "You know how moms are."

By now the group had reached the base of the tree. "Mrs. Burke?"

"Hello, Mr. Randolph. How are you?"

She could tell that he resisted the impulse to smile, but with difficulty. "Fine. How are you?"

"I'm fine," she said, casually brushing a wisp of hair out of her eyes. For all her composure, they could be chatting over the rose-bush hedge that separated their property.

"Do you need any help?"

"I think I can manage, thank you. I'm sorry my children involved you."

"Glad to be of service." She watched his brows draw together. "Are you sure you can make it all right?"

Elizabeth glanced down at the ground. It tilted to a precarious angle. "F—fairly sure."

He seemed doubtful. For a moment he said nothing, then, as though reaching a decision, he said, "Grab that branch—no, the other one—with your right hand. That's it. Now move your left foot . . . yeah, there."

Instructing her in a masculine voice that reminded her of far-off and friendly thunder, he talked her down. She had almost made it when they all heard the sound of ripping cloth.

"Oh!" She was on the lowest branch, about to place her foot on the stepladder when she was brought up short.

"What was that?" Thad asked.

"It's . . . uh, I think something got caught on the tree limb."

"What?"

"One of those frilly things," Matt informed him helpfully. "She wears all that lacy junk under her clothes."

"Matthew!" Elizabeth's cheeks went up in flames. She hoped her neighbor thought the deep blush that covered her face was caused by her strenuous, and so far unsuccessful, attempts to unsnag her petticoat from the branch.

"Here, I'd better do it." Thad stepped to the top of the ladder.

"I can do it."

"No, you'd better concentrate on holding on with both hands. I'm afraid you're going to fall."

Glancing down at the ground, which seemed to recede the closer she got to it, Elizabeth did as she was told and held on for dear life while her bachelor-stranger-neighbor of the gray hair and broad shoulders flipped back her taupe twill skirt and buried his hands in yards of linen and lace looking for the hangup. It seemed to take forever for him to find it.

"There," he said finally, "found it." He fingered the ripped material. "It only made a little tear. Maybe you can mend it."

"Yes, maybe," Elizabeth said, gently tugging the lacy hem of her petticoat from between his fingers. "Thank you."

Standing on the ladder, his face was brought up almost to a level even with hers. Elizabeth had never been this close to him. Never before close enough to see that his eyes were very blue. Never before close enough to notice that his hair wasn't totally gray, but salt and pepper, heavy on the salt. Never before close enough to smell his cologne which made her think of saddles and sex. And seeing his fingers rubbing a hapless strand of torn lace between them had made her eyeballs catch fire and her mouth go dry.

"You're welcome," he said quietly. His eyes remained steadily on hers. "You're shaking, you know. Let me help you down."

He stepped to the ground and moved the ladder aside. Then, reaching up, he grasped her around the waist. His wide hands settled on either side of it. She felt his strong fingers fold around her waist, almost meeting at her spine. "Put your hands on my shoulders and lean forward. I'll do the rest."

Blindly, Elizabeth obeyed. The cloth of his shirt felt soothing against her scraped palms as she tentatively laid them on his shoulders. Her hands looked very small and feminine there. Squeezing her waist slightly, he lifted her from the branch. She landed against him and threw him slightly off balance. His arms wrapped around her. He staggered back a few steps, taking her with him.

His chest was as solid as a wall. All of him was. He made her feel slight and fragile. Her senses reeled.

Nonsense. She was still dizzy from the height, that was all. But why couldn't she feel the ground?

Because she wasn't touching it, that's why. He was holding her high against him. Slowly, he lowered her until her feet touched the cool grass. Her breasts dragged against his chest. For a split second, the notch of her thighs caught on the fly of his trousers.

A tidal wave of heat surged through her.

"Okay now?" he asked.

Far from okay, she nodded.

His hands dropped from her waist. She took a step back, putting space between them. When she risked raising her head and looking up at him, she saw mirrored in his eyes a woman rosily flushed with arousal.

Then she was startled to realize that the woman was herself.

Two

"Gee, Mom, your eyes look weird."

Matt's piping voice dispelled Elizabeth's momentary trance. Nervously, she flattened her hand against the base of her throat where her heart was beating wildly. "I, uh, I guess climbing the tree was scarier than I thought it would be. How's Baby?"

"Much better," Megan said. The kitten was curled against the girl's narrow chest. "She's purring."

Elizabeth knew the feeling. She was purring too. Humming. Churning. Whatever. She hadn't felt like this since . . . It had been so long since she'd felt this giddy, she couldn't even remember it. But then it had been a long time since she'd been touched by a man.

She avoided looking at her neighbor again until she had no choice but to lift her gaze back to Thad Randolph's. Through the thick twilight, his eyes shone piercingly blue beneath dense eyebrows which had remained dark in spite of his graying hair.

Elizabeth swallowed with difficulty. "Thank you for helping me out of the tree, Mr. Randolph."

He smiled. He had very nice teeth, she noticed. Straight and white. "You're welcome. Please call me Thad, though."

Again she saw herself mirrored in his eyes. Her hair was disheveled, framing her face with fine, pale tendrils. Her blouse was hopelessly dirty and there was a smudge of grime on her chin. She looked frightful and had made a complete fool out of herself. No doubt he would enjoy telling all his buddies the story of the nutty widow who lived in the house behind his. When he got to the part about her petticoat and what Matt had said, he'd smile lecherously, intimating that the tale only got better from there, but discretion prevented him from telling all.

"Come along, children," she said as briskly as an English nanny rounding up her charges. "It's getting dark. Time we went inside. Matt, please put the ladder back in the garage."

"Why do I have to?" he whined. "I got the ladder out. Make Megan put it up."

"I'm taking care of Baby," Megan protested.

"It's my turn to take care of Baby. You think she's your kitten, but she's not."

"I asked if we could have her."

"Yeah, but she's mine too."

"Mostly mine."

"*Uh-huh!* She belongs to both of us, doesn't she, Mom?"

Elizabeth had come to expect this kind of squabbling, and usually tuned it out. Tonight, however, it clipped the tenuous threads of her patience.

"Will you both stop bickering and do as I say?" As if getting herself caught in a tree weren't enough, her children chose now to behave their worst in front of the neighbor.

"Before you go inside, I'd like to show you something."

All three turned at the sound of Thad Randolph's peacemaking voice. "In my garage." He smiled at Elizabeth. "Something the kids will enjoy seeing."

"The puppies?" Megan asked in a hushed voice. "Did they get borned?"

"Last night. Four of them."

"Oh, Mom, can we go see them?"

Elizabeth was helplessly trapped. While she appreciated Thad's conciliatory gesture, she also resented his interference in a family squabble. But for her to refuse to let her children see the litter would be unthinkable. Not even moms could be that cruel. "You can see them as soon as you take the ladder back into the garage." There. She hadn't surrendered unconditionally.

Matt dashed off, ladder in tow. Unbelievably Megan went with him and held the door open.

"You don't mind, do you?"

Elizabeth turned toward Thad. "Of course not. They've been telling me that your setter was about to have her puppies." Until now she had never realized how tall he was. The top of her head didn't quite reach his chin. "I just hope they don't upset the new mother."

"Penny is the most docile dog I've ever had. And she adores your children."

Elizabeth clasped her hands at her waist, an unconscious nervous gesture. "They don't disturb you, do they? It seems as if they're always in your yard. I've told them to stay out of it, but—"

"They don't bother me at all. In fact, I get a kick out of watching them play."

A thousand questions flocked to her mind—did he

have any children of his own? If not, why not? If he did, were they living with his ex-wife? *Was* there an ex-wife? Or was he, like herself, widowed?

Even if she'd had the opportunity to satisfy her curiosity and ask such personal questions, she wouldn't have. But she didn't have the opportunity. Matt and Megan came racing back, breathless, eyes alight, their cheeks ruddy with excitement.

"I put Baby in the house in case she did something to scare the puppies," Megan said.

"Let's go."

Thad turned in the direction of his detached garage. All the houses on the block had been built in the thirties. It had become fashionable about ten years before for young families to buy these houses and renovate them, as John and Elizabeth Burke had done. The two children ran ahead, chasing between the shade trees in the large connecting lots.

"Be careful not to touch the puppies," Elizabeth called after them. "And come right back."

"Aren't you coming?" Thad stopped and turned around.

"I—uh—was I supposed to?" she stammered. "I mean, did you want me to?"

"Sure. Come on. Who could resist looking at a litter of puppies?"

And what woman could resist his eyes, Elizabeth asked herself.

He extended his hand, but she didn't take it. She did, however, fall into step beside him, surreptitiously tucking fugitive strands of hair back into the slipping knot on the back of her head.

This whole scene had become bizarre. She hadn't put her shoes back on and was still in her stockings. The grass felt damp and cold against the soles of her feet. They'd had the first frost last week and leaves had begun to fall. Occasionally she'd step on one and it would crunch beneath her instep. The sun had slid quickly beneath the horizon. The adjoining backyards were deep in violet shadows. She felt compelled to make conversation, but it was difficult to find a topic they had in common. At last she hit on one.

"I like the color you painted the trim on your house."

"Thanks. It took me long enough to paint it all."

"You've got a lot of trim."

"And I hate to paint."

"Luckily the house had been redone when you bought it." He'd been living there six months or so. She couldn't remember exactly when he'd moved in.

"I wouldn't have bought it otherwise."

They had reached the back door of his garage. He opened it and stood aside to let her go first. Self-consciously, she squeezed past him through the door. The hem of her skirt brushed against his legs. Cloth dragged against cloth, like a wave reluctant to recede from the shore.

It was dark inside the garage because the large door facing the street and driveway was closed. Only one dim electric bulb burned over the bed Thad had made for his Irish setter and her litter. It smelled musty and musky inside. Inexplicably, Elizabeth was reminded of her stable fantasy.

Despite her instructions for them not to touch the puppies for fear the dam wouldn't like it, her children were crawling over the pile of old blankets, petting the new mother and her babies. Elizabeth was afraid that in their excitement Megan and Matt would crush one of the puppies. Again she cautioned them to be careful.

"They're all right," Thad said. He nudged her elbow with his hand, urging her forward.

"Can we hold one, Mom? Pleeeeze," Megan begged.

"I don't know," she replied uncertainly. The setter looked benign enough, but new mothers could be fiercely protective.

"I don't think Penny will mind. If you're very careful," Thad said.

Gently each child held one of the tiny pups. They oohed and aahed over them. Elizabeth found herself doing the same. Thad had been right. Who could resist a new puppy?

"Oh, they *are* darling, aren't they?" she whispered, kneeling down to get a closer look. The Irish setter, Penny, was basking in their attention and didn't seem to be at all nettled by the children.

"Want to hold one?"

Elizabeth looked at Thad from across the pile of old blankets where the new family lay. He was kneeling on one knee, the other was raised and bent. The single light bulb cast one side of his face into shadow and lit individual strands of his hair, particularly the silver ones. He had a well-lived-in face, but it was handsome and strong. His face said that he was a man of high integrity and steadfast conviction. He wouldn't provoke a fight, but he would find it untenable to turn the other cheek.

There were traces of pain in his features. And sensitivity. And sensuality. Especially around his beautifully fashioned mouth. It was saved from being pretty by the vertical grooves parenthesizing it. The rest of him was uncompromisingly male.

Elizabeth's chest grew full and heavy. Her mouth went dry. In answer to his question, she nodded. Very gently, he scooped one of the puppies in his large hand and lifted it away from its mother's teat. The puppy protested with a querulous squeak that caused them all to laugh. Thad laid the soft, warm ball into the bowl of Elizabeth's waiting hands.

She raised the puppy to her cheek and rubbed it against her skin. "He is—It *is* a he, isn't it?"

Chuckling, Thad nodded. "I think so. Three males, one female."

"You can tell by looking at their bellies," Matt said, puffed up with his superior knowledge on the subject. "The boys have penises."

"Oh, gross!" Megan shivered. She lifted the puppy she was holding over her head and glanced at its underside. Satisfied that she was holding the female, she continued to hug it gently.

Elizabeth cleared her throat loudly. She could feel Thad's laughing eyes on her. "He's so soft," she murmured, still allowing the puppy to root against her cheek.

"Do you like 'em, Mom?" Matt asked.

"Of course I do. They're beautiful."

"Can we have one?"

"Matthew!" Hadn't she taught her child better manners than that?

"Please?"

"Can we, Mom?" Megan chimed in.

"No."

"How come?"

"Because we just got Baby. No more pets."

"We'll take care of it, honest."

"I said no."

"But, Mom—"

"Whoa, Matt," Thad interrupted. "The litter is already spoken for."

"All of 'em?" the boy asked mournfully.

"Yep. Sorry, friend."

"That's okay," Matt mumbled, keeping his head down.

Thad placed his finger beneath the dejected chin and tilted it up. "Maybe by the time Penny has another litter, we'll have your mom talked into you having one, okay?"

The boy's face brightened. "Okay!" He returned the puppy he was holding to its mother. "I'm going to tell Tim that I got to see the puppies first and that the next time Penny has babies, I'm getting one." He couldn't wait to lord that over his best friend.

"Wait for me." Megan returned the female pup to its mother and they both ran for the door to the garage.

"Watch for cars when you cross the street," Elizabeth called. "And be home in five minutes. It's time for dinner."

"Okay, Mom." The door slammed shut behind them.

Elizabeth looked at Thad and smiled helplessly. "Where did I go wrong?"

He laughed at her chagrin. "You haven't gone wrong. They're great kids. Just energetic." Still smiling, he stroked Penny's head. The dog worshipfully licked the back of his hand.

The slamming door had had the impact of a thunderbolt, leaving a vibrating silence in its place. The garage suddenly seemed a private, intimate enclosure. The stillness made Elizabeth feel awkward. Except for a few words exchanged at a distance, she'd just met this man. Being alone with him was unsettling.

"I'd better get home and start dinner." Leaning forward, she laid the puppy close to its mother. He nuzzled and found an available place at which to nurse.

As Elizabeth withdrew her hands, Thad surprised her by reaching across the dam and her litter and grasping them. He turned her palms up toward the light. "What did you do to your hands?"

The shock of his touch almost cost her the power of speech. "The tree. I scraped them on the bark," she finally choked out.

"As soon as you get home, you'd better wash them in a disinfectant soap and put some ointment on them."

"Yes, I will."

His lips twisted into a lopsided grin of self-derision. "Who am I to give first-aid advice to a mother of two, huh?"

She smiled in return, but disengaged her hands, hopefully without appearing to be in a hurry to. But she was. She barely curbed the impulse to fold her arms across her chest and tuck her hands into her armpits, as though ashamed of them for committing some grievous transgression. They were tingling and it wasn't entirely from having been scraped on the tree.

He stood up when she did and together they walked toward the door. "I didn't know you had a motorcycle," she observed, grateful at a chance to break the silence. A motorcycle was parked in one half of the double garage.

"Yeah, I bought it when I got back from Nam. I don't have time to ride it much, mostly on weekends, but I enjoy it."

Nam? Had he been a soldier? "You don't seem the type for a motorcycle."

He paused with his hand on the doorknob. "The

type? You're not one of those ultraconservatives who thinks that anyone sitting astride a motorcycle is degenerate, are you?"

"Of course not."

"Good. Maybe you can go riding with me sometime. If you'd like to."

"Oh, I don't think so," she said quickly, looking dubiously at the cycle. "I don't think I'd like sitting astride. A motorcycle."

There was enough time and space between her two sentences to let inquisitiveness dawn and mature in his eyes. For a moment that blue gaze held hers. "Don't knock it till you've tried it."

Studying his face, she gauged his intention and decided that if his words carried a double meaning, she was better off ignoring it. "The children will be looking for me," she said uncomfortably.

He held open the door. She stepped through it into the evening air, which had become chilly. But she welcomed the bracing cold. It helped clear her head. She hugged herself for warmth, and also to prevent him from seeing her nipples. They were erect beneath her blouse. If he noticed that, he'd think—

"I like all that lacy junk you wear under your clothes."

"What?" Stumbling in the damp grass, she spun around.

He was smiling disarmingly. "I don't think it's junk. I was only quoting Matt." He looked her up and down in the arrogant, possessive, masculine manner that Adam had first used in the Garden of Eden and that no amount of legislation was ever going to outlaw. "Unisex clothing they can keep. I enjoy looking at a woman who dresses like one."

"Thank you."

"Do you always wear soft things?" he asked, nodding down toward her blouse and the nipples that were tenting it.

She moistened her lips with her tongue. "I like wearing feminine clothes. Besides that, it's good for my business."

"That's right, you sell lingerie in your shop, don't you?" At her surprised expression, he explained, "One day when I was in the Cavanaugh, I saw you through the window of Fantasy."

"Oh."

Her first reaction was surprise that he knew about her business. The next was to wonder what had brought him to the Hotel Cavanaugh. The third was to chide herself for being so naïve.

Scores of discreet affairs went on in the well-appointed rooms every day. Why else would a man as attractive as Thad Randolph be walking across the lobby of the Hotel Cavanaugh in the middle of the day? And it had to have been during the day because she wasn't open late. The hotel restaurants were good, but there were others in the city that were just as good and less expensive for lunch. Chances were that he'd gone to the hotel to satisfy another appetite.

"Before I knew the name of your shop, I'd always wondered what significance your license plate had."

"My sister's idea," Elizabeth told him absently.

Had the woman he'd met at the Cavanaugh been hired for the afternoon? Or was she a housewife hopelessly in love with the wrong man? Or a career woman looking for kicks to relieve the pressure of her job?

What difference did it make to *her*? Piqued at her own curiosity, she said, "The next time you're in the hotel, drop in and say hello."

"Thanks. I will. I might even buy something. Your merchandise looked . . . interesting."

Was it a trick of the wavering shadows or did his eyes move down to her breasts once more?

"Well, thanks again for helping me out of the tree."

"My pleasure."

Again, his words caused a warm tide to spill through her. For that very reason she gave him a verbal cold shoulder. "Good night, Mr. Randolph."

"Good night, Elizabeth."

He had deliberately used her first name after she'd avoided using his. Nodding brusquely, she quickly crossed his yard into her own. At the sycamore, she retrieved her shoes but didn't even pause to put them on as she made her way toward her back door. Only when it was safely closed behind her did she breathe a sigh of relief. But the respite didn't last long. She heard her children coming through the front door.

"Mom?"

"In here." She dropped her shoes on the floor and padded toward the refrigerator. Thank goodness Mrs. Alder had remembered to take a pound of ground chuck out of the freezer. It was thawed.

"What's for supper?" Megan asked as she came through the door connecting the kitchen to the rest of the house.

"Hamburgers."

"Can I light the grill this time?" Matt asked.

"No, I'm frying the meat tonight."

"Aw, Mom, they taste so much better when you cook them outside."

"Not tonight."

"How come?"

Brother! Did she ever get sick of that question.

"Because I'm the mother and I said so. Now go wash up, then come back and set the table."

They slunk out, muttering about her unfairness. Elizabeth's mouth watered at the thought of meat cooked over charcoal, but she wasn't about to go back outside tonight. All summer, she had been uncomfortably aware of Thad Randolph sitting on his screened back porch watching TV until late every night. Each time she had to go outdoors, she debated with herself. Should she call out a greeting, as she did to all her other neighbors? Should she give him a tentative little wave? It was nerve-wracking, this never knowing what to do.

If he hadn't seen her, she didn't want him to think she was trying to attract his attention. And if he had seen her, she didn't want him to know that she knew he had. So it had always seemed prudent just to ignore him.

Her behavior was juvenile at best and rude at worst, but a widow couldn't be too careful with her reputation. At the risk of being unfriendly, Elizabeth had been unapproachable to the opposite sex since her husband's death two years earlier.

She had waved John good-bye on his way out the back door that morning, never suspecting it would be the last time she would see him alive. In fact, she'd been distracted by Megan, who had just remembered that she needed a spool of thread and a paper plate for an art project at school. Elizabeth hadn't even noticed what shirt and necktie he had on that day. She hadn't realized that he needed a haircut until she'd gone to the morgue to identify his body, which had been pulled from the wreckage of the freeway pileup. It took her days to recall their last private conversation. Their last kiss. The last time they'd made love.

What she would always remember was his smile and his laugh, his kindness and caring, his sweet lovemaking and his dreams for their future. He had been a darling man who had given her two beautiful children and a great deal of happiness. His death had left a vacancy in her heart that would never be filled.

That gaping wound was bothering her more than usual tonight. That's why when she tucked in Megan and Matt, she drew them to her and hugged them so tight they became embarrassed by her emotion and squirmed free.

Her ardent hugs represented more than her love for her children. They indicated her desperate need for human contact, for intimacy of any kind. She missed being on the receiving end of someone's love and affection. A grownup's love and affection. A man's. Sometimes her body and soul were so hungry for it, she thought she'd die.

Once the lights were out in the rest of the house, she entered her own bedroom and switched on the floor lamp. It stood beside her bed on a brass pole and had a glass shade shaped like a lotus blossom. She'd redecorated the bedroom several months after John's death because it held too many poignant memories.

Now, it was arranged just the way she wanted it, but she could find no joy in it. A beautiful room should be shared. Her boudoir might just as well be a cloister. Lilah was right. Living a nun's life was no fun unless you were a nun. Going to bed alone every night was nothing to look forward to. She missed the comfort of having a warm body lying against hers while she slept.

But what could a decent widow with two children

looking to her for moral guidance do about her celibacy? Nothing. Contrary to Lilah's advice, she couldn't rush out and net a man just to cool the fevers of her body. Would that one could take a pill to eliminate sexual urges the way aspirin staved off fever.

Thanks to Lilah's half-baked psychology, her mind had run amok today. She had behaved like a total idiot in front of Thad . . . Mr. Randolph . . . this evening. He was probably over there now laughing at how flustered she'd become when he rescued her from the tree.

Impatient with herself for acting like such a simpering ninny over a nice pair of shoulders and blue eyes that would give Paul Newman's competition, she turned off the lamp and got into bed. But she couldn't resist the temptation to peep through the slats of her shutters to see if his lights were still on.

Yes. She could see him through the screened walls surrounding his porch. He was slumped in an easy chair, staring into the silver, flickering TV screen. He was alone too. And she wondered if his solitude was by choice, or if he hated loneliness as much as she did.

"And then what happened?"

"And then he had to reach up there and lift her down."

"Mr. Randolph did?"

"Uh-huh. He put his hands . . . here."

"But that was after her petticoat got torn."

"Oh, yeah, I forgot about that."

"Her petticoat got torn? You skipped that part. Go back to that."

"Good morning."

Three heads turned at the sound of Elizabeth's

sleepy-hoarse voice. Knotting the belt of her chenille robe, which was way past retirement age, she shot her sister a poisonous look and headed for the coffeepot.

"Why didn't you wake me up?" she asked, stirring Sweet'n Low into black coffee.

"Because it sounds as though you needed a good night's rest." Wearing a feline smile, Lilah bit into a piece of crisp bacon.

"I see you've already had breakfast." On the round kitchen table were three syrup-sticky plates.

"I fixed pancakes for the kids. Want some?"

"No," Elizabeth snapped ungraciously. Ordinarily she would have been grateful for Lilah's dropping by to cook breakfast for Megan and Matt so she could sleep late. On Saturdays she kept Fantasy open only from noon until five. It was her one morning a week to sleep past six-thirty. "Go do your chores," she told her children crossly. "Make your beds and put all your dirty clothes in the hamper."

"Then can I go out and play?"

"Yes." Breaking her first smile of the day, Elizabeth swatted Matt on the seat as he sped past her chair. Deferring to Megan's maturity, she gave her a brief hug.

"Cute kids," Lilah remarked when they were alone.

"And talkative. Especially when they've got a busybody pumping them for information."

"I didn't pump," Lilah said righteously. "I merely asked what was new and they told me." She propped her elbows on the table and leaned forward. "Did the mysterious Mr. Randolph *really* rescue you from the tree last night?"

There was no use denying it. "Yes, he did."

"Bingo!" Lilah chortled, clapping her hands together.

"It was no big deal. Not nearly as melodramatic as you're making it sound."

"We were just getting to the good part when you came in. What was that about the torn petticoat?"

"Nothing. My petticoat got caught on a twig."

"And he got it off?" Lilah's smile was downright lascivious.

"Yes, but it was a humiliating experience. I felt like a fool."

"What's he like? What'd he say?"

"Forget it, Lilah. He's . . . he's elderly."

"Elderly?"

"Well, you yourself noticed that he has gray hair. He's too old for me."

Lilah frowned. "How gray? How old?"

"I don't know. I didn't ask," she said peevishly.

"Hmm, well, it's a start. At least you attracted his attention."

"I didn't do it on purpose."

"The net result is the same."

"Get this through your conniving head, there is no 'net result.' "

"Stop shouting at me, Elizabeth. I'm interested for your sake."

"Well, don't be!"

Lilah sat back in her chair, sighing in exasperation. "Brother! You're as cranky as an old bear this morning. Know what I think? I think you'd be in a much better mood if he'd spent more time unsnagging your petticoat."

"Lilah," Elizabeth said warningly.

Lilah was unfazed. "Here, read this while I'm doing the dishes." She tossed a magazine toward Elizabeth before she began clearing the table. It was a popular monthly publication which had an enormous female reading audience. "Page ten."

Elizabeth thumbed forward to the specified page. Upon reading the headline of the advertisement, she glanced up at her sister, a glance Lilah pointedly disregarded.

By the time Elizabeth had read the lengthy ad, Lilah had rinsed and placed all the dishes in the dishwasher. She returned to the table. The two sisters stared at one another.

"Well?" Lilah said at last.

"Well?"

"What do you think of the idea?"

"You're not serious? You expect me to write out my fantasies for publication?"

"I do."

"You're sick."

"I'm normal. And so are you. And so are your fantasies. Only I'll bet they're much more detailed and romantic than most. What could be the harm in writing them down and submitting them for the book this publisher is putting together?"

"The harm?" Elizabeth cried. "The harm could be that I have two children."

"They won't be buying a copy, will they?"

"Don't be cute, Lilah. Your idea is absurd. I'd never feel comfortable about doing something like this. I'm a mother. A widow."

"But you're hardly Granny Grunt. You're a young, attractive woman whose husband happened to die prematurely. It says right here that they want stories from 'average' women. You qualify. The only thing that's not average about you is your love life, which is zilch. But," she added hastily when she saw that Elizabeth was about to take issue, "it can be a bonus. If you're deprived, then your fantasies should really sizzle."

Elizabeth rolled her eyes heavenward. "I can't do it. I don't know where you ever came up with the hare-brained notion I could."

"Look," Lilah said, flattening her hand on the table, "you write the fantasies, as many as you want. I'll do the rest. I'll submit them under a pen name. You'll remain anonymous. I'll do everything but cash the check the publisher sends you when your manuscripts are selected."

"Check?"

"Didn't you read that paragraph?"

"I didn't get that far."

"There." Lilah pointed to that part of the text. "They're paying two hundred and fifty dollars for each fantasy they select to go in the book no matter how long or short it is, historical or contemporary, first person or whatever."

In spite of herself, Elizabeth's interest was piqued. It had taken virtually all of John's life-insurance money and their savings for her to open Fantasy. From the beginning, the shop in the well-trafficked lobby of the Hotel Cavanaugh had made a profit, but a small one. She wasn't destitute, but she couldn't afford extravagances. As the children grew older they became more expensive. She'd often worried about how she would finance their college educations.

On the other hand, earning money by writing out her most secret fantasies seemed like a disreputable thing to do. "I'm not a writer."

"How do you know? Have you ever tried? You always made A's in English. Besides, from what I understand ninety-nine percent of writing is imagination. You've got gobs of that. Lizzie," Lilah said, warming to her subject. "this is something you've been preparing for all your life. No one daydreams more than you. It's time you converted that pastime into an enterprise."

"I couldn't."

"Why not? It will remain our little secret, just like the time we glued Grandma's house shoes to the closet floor."

"As I recall that was your bright idea too. And *I* got a spanking for going along."

"The hilarity was worth the spanking," Lilah said with a dismissive shrug.

Elizabeth sighed, knowing that Lilah never took no for an answer. "I don't have the time to write even if I wanted to."

"What else do you do at night?"

She had a point and Elizabeth conceded it. She left the table and moved to the coffeemaker on the counter. "I'd be embarrassed for anybody to read my fantasies."

"Good! That means they're hot and juicy. That's just what they want. See? 'Explicit, but tasteful,' " she read from the magazine. "That means make them good and dirty, but not crude."

"I think that lost something in your translation."

"Well, are you going to do it or not?"

"I'm not. If you're so high on the idea, why don't you do it?"

"Because I don't have your creativity. When we played make-believe, you always made up the scenarios. I only acted out the parts."

She could feel herself weakening. It would be a catharsis of sorts, wouldn't it? A way of venting her sexual frustration. A challenge she needed. Something to do that was hers and hers alone. Not something she was doing for her children or for her business, but for herself, the woman. She had so few personal indulgences.

"I don't know, Lilah," she said, unready to capitulate entirely. "It seems so . . . so . . ."

Her voice trailed off as she spied something across her yard. Thad Randolph was nailing together lumber and wiring to form what looked like a pen. Probably for the puppies. Matt was assisting him by holding the nails. Megan, sitting in the old swing which a former owner of Thad's house had suspended from the branch of an oak, was giving advice. Baby was napping on Megan's lap.

But what captivated and held Elizabeth's attention was the man. His shirt was unbuttoned to reveal a sturdy chest and flat stomach. Patches of dark, curly hair grew in strategic places. The supple muscles of his arms and shoulders contracted and relaxed each time he moved. A lock of sweat-damp hair had fallen over his brow. He laughed at something Matt said. When he did, he threw back his head and revealed a strong, tanned throat. As he stood up and brushed sawdust off his jeans, Elizabeth couldn't help but notice how they clung to his thighs.

"What's the matter?" Lilah moved up behind her and peered through the window over the sink. Elizabeth heard her sister's gasp. For several moments, they stared at Thad Randolph until he heaved the contraption to his shoulder and carried it into his garage. Matt and Megan trooped after him.

Elizabeth turned her back to her sister and busied herself with pouring another cup of coffee.

"Elderly, huh?" Lilah said wryly.

"I told you I couldn't guess his age."

"Lizzie, men who look like that don't *age*, they *ripen*. Looking like that, what the hell difference does it make if he's fifty? A hundred and fifty?"

"It makes absolutely no difference to me. A vital point which seems to escape you."

"What color are his eyes?"

"Sort of blue." Sort of sparkling, shimmering, sapphire blue.

"What does he do for a living?"

"He, uh, owns a cement company, I think. That's what one of the neighbors told me when he moved in. His Jeep has the name stenciled on the side."

Lilah snapped her fingers. "Randolph Concrete. Sure. His trucks are on every construction site in town. He must make a bundle."

"Mother always taught us it was vulgar to discuss someone's finances."

Lilah had stopped worrying about what their mother considered vulgar years ago. She was unabashedly gazing out the window in hopes of catching sight of him again. "Did you see the way he handled his tool?"

Elizabeth's head snapped around and Lilah giggled. "Gotcha! I was thinking about his hammer. What were you thinking about?"

"What you're thinking is all wrong," Elizabeth said with asperity.

"And what's that?"

"That there's a romance brewing across our backyards. He's a nice man. He's patient with my children."

"A real tribute considering his *advanced age*," Lilah said sarcastically. "Don't they disturb him during his afternoon nap?"

Elizabeth glared at her. "Frankly I'm grateful for the time he spends with Matt particularly. He needs a man's influence. But it stops there, Lilah. I could never be attracted to a man like Mr. Randolph."

"Have you checked your pulse lately? If he doesn't attract you, you're dead."

Elizabeth sighed. "He's not my type. He's too . . . physical. Too large . . ."

"Um-hum." Lilah smacked her lips.

Elizabeth made a supreme effort to ignore that too. "I could never go for a hard-hat type."

Lilah grinned wickedly. "I'll bet his hat isn't all that's hard."

"Oh! Will you go wallow in the gutter? I'm sure your mind would enjoy the company." Lilah only laughed at her. "And you can forget about my writing down any fantasies for publication. I don't even have any fantasies!"

Three

The figures blurred in front of her eyes again. Impatiently Elizabeth tossed down her pencil and gave up trying to concentrate on Fantasy's financial records. It was Monday morning. The shop had been open only half an hour. So far she'd had no customers. She was catching up on some bookkeeping while waiting for Mr. Adam Cavanaugh to arrive. She'd been notified that he would be circulating through the hotel later that day.

But every time she tried to review the profit and loss columns in front of her, her mind began to wander. It kept going back to the discussion Lilah and she had had the previous Saturday morning. Her sister had planted a seed in the fertile field of her brain, and it had germinated in spite of her wishes that it whither and die.

If an interrogator had shoved slivers of bamboo under her fingernails, Elizabeth wouldn't have admitted writing out her stable fantasy in the privacy of her bedroom late Saturday night. She'd toyed with the tempting idea all through the McDonald's dinner and Disney movie she'd treated her children to that evening. On the outside chance that she might see Thad Randolph, she hadn't wanted to hang around the house. She'd kept the kids out as late as possible and was miffed to see that his Jeep wasn't parked in his driveway when they finally did get home.

The outing had still been well worth the effort. The kids had loved the classic animated film. They'd individually thanked her for taking them when she kissed them good night. But as always when she went into her room, undressed, and got into bed, she was alone.

It was then that she had taken a spiral notebook out of the drawer in her nightstand and begun to write down the word pictures her mind was constantly painting. She became lost in the effort. The words seemed to appear on the paper through no volition of her own. They flowed freely from the pen as though it were as magical as the wand in the fairy tale she'd just seen.

Descriptions of the characters, their clothing, the setting, all came easily because she envisioned them so clearly. But some words she found difficult to write. Words which she would never have occasion to speak aloud. Anatomical parts for instance, or words with blatantly sexual connotations. But she penned them nonetheless. By the time she put a period at the end of the last sentence, her body was damp with perspiration and her heart was thumping in a lovemaking rhythm.

Laying her pen aside, she flipped back through the pages and read what she had written. After reading the final word, she threw off the bed covers, ripped the pages out of the notebook, and destroyed them in the bathroom.

Her fantasy had sounded dopey. Lilah was insane and she was insane for ever listening to her. Agitated with herself, she returned to bed and snapped off the lamp. She tried to sleep, squeezing her eyes shut so tightly she got a headache from the effort. Tossing and turning, she tried to convince herself that the fantasy she had written had been so bad as to be unreadable. But that wasn't true. She'd ripped it up because it had been so good.

She had lived with herself for twenty-nine years and had never guessed what a dirty mind she had!

Fantasy was closed on Sundays. That afternoon she'd taken the children on a picnic in the municipal park to keep them occupied and away from the house. When they left, Thad had been out pruning shrubs.

"Can Thad come on the picnic too?" Matt had asked her as she shepherded him into the car.

"Thad's busy."

"He pro'bly wouldn't be busy if we asked him to come on the picnic."

"We aren't going to ask him."

"We've got plenty of food."

"He can have some of mine," Megan offered.

Elizabeth climbed behind the steering wheel and quickly started the car to end the argument. The picnic had been successful. But while the children played on the jungle gym, Elizabeth sat on a park bench and analyzed the fantasy she'd written the night before. She thought of ways to change and improve it. Then she would remember that it no longer existed and was a closed issue. She forced herself to forget it.

Well, now it was Monday. She had work to do. The owner of the hotel chain was due to arrive at any minute. And she still hadn't forgotten the erotic dream she'd committed to paper. She was preoccupied with her fantasy and her troublesome neighbor.

Although *that* was the trouble, he wasn't troublesome. She couldn't fault him for anything. As neighbors went, he was perfect. He could have been a real hell-raising bachelor who had women constantly parading through his house. He could host drunken orgies that would keep her up nights. He could be ornery about the noise her children made when they played in the backyard. The motorcycle seemed a bit out of character. She suspected that he was no angel, but at least she didn't have to contend with a party animal.

Of course he could have been more modest than to leave his shirt unbuttoned when he was working outside in his yard. On the other hand, he might not have been wearing a shirt at all. What if he'd been shirtless when the emergency with Baby occurred? What if his arms and their bunching biceps had been bare when he reached up for her and encircled her waist with his strong hands? What if she'd had to touch his naked shoulders and be pressed against that broad, hairy chest and flat, corrugated stomach? What if—

"Mrs. Burke?"

Elizabeth jumped as though she'd been shot and whirled around to see that a group of people had congregated just inside the door of her shop. They were staring at her curiously and she wondered how many times the man had spoken her name before rousing her.

"Yes?" she said, breathless with embarrassment.

"Hello. I'm Adam Cavanaugh."

The dark-haired, dark-eyed man who was crossing the plush carpet, hand extended, was heart-stoppingly handsome. Impeccably dressed in a well-tailored three-piece pin-striped business suit, he still managed to look as dashing as a Caribbean pirate. That reckless flare was in his smile, which was wide, white, and friendly, and in his coffee-colored eyes, which twinkled with amusement, as though he knew he had caught her red-handed in a naughty daydream. He clasped Elizabeth's hand in a firm handshake.

"Mr. Cavanaugh, it's a pleasure to meet you in person." She congratulated herself for not stammering, which, under the circumstances, was a real feat.

"The same goes for me." He released her hand and looked about the shop. Turning to his entourage of yes-men, who respectfully lurked in his aura, he nodded with apparent satisfaction. "The photographs I was sent didn't do Fantasy justice." His dark eyes swung back to Elizabeth. "I love it."

"Thank you."

"Wherever did you get the idea?"

She shrugged self-consciously. "I've always liked beautiful things. Feminine things. When I decided to go into business for myself, that's what I wanted to sell. I tried to think of a suitable location for such a shop, where there would be men buying presents for their . . . ladies. At that time, Hotel Cavanaugh was still under construction." She smiled up at him. "It seemed a natural."

"Very intuitive."

"I'm glad you saw the same potential that I did and accepted the proposal I sent you."

"Actually I can't take the credit for approving your idea. I have lessee managers who handle that. However, I couldn't be more pleased that they decided in your favor."

She was appalled at her naïveté. Adam Cavanaugh was far too important and busy to concern himself with each and every lessee. She felt herself blushing.

"I'm sure your appearance boosts your sales, Mrs. Burke." Without compunction, Cavanaugh studied her face and hairdo. The chignon was loose and wispy enough to suggest that it had been mussed. Perhaps by a man's caressing hands. "You certainly look the part."

Elizabeth grew warm beneath his appraising stare. "I brewed some spiced tea." She hoped to remove his attention from her by indicating a simmering silver pot and a collection of porcelain cups sitting on a small round table covered with a lace tablecloth. "Would you like to sample some of the chocolates I sell?"

"I'll pass on the tea, but the chocolates, by all means," he said with a brilliant smile which was almost boyish.

Not only was Adam Cavanaugh incredibly handsome, he was likable. He chatted with Elizabeth while the lackeys in his entourage sipped tea and munched down almost fifty dollars' worth of chocolates. The entrepreneur seemed genuinely interested in her. When she mentioned her children, he quizzed her about them at length and paid close attention to her answers. It was little wonder why this man was so successful. He was a good listener and made the speaker feel that what he had to say was important, interesting, and entertaining.

He took her hand again and pressed it between his. "I'll be in and out of the city for the next few weeks," he told her. "I want us to get together for a private meeting. Can that be arranged?"

"Certainly," Elizabeth replied with more composure than she felt. His touch was that of a man who touched women frequently, who knew how, and who enjoyed it.

"I'll look forward to it, then."

He retained her hand for several seconds before saying good-bye and turning toward the door. He was brought up short at the sight of the woman standing on the threshold. She had on tight black leather pants tucked into knee-high boots. A long fringed paisley shawl had been tossed over a black turtleneck sweater. Gold disk earrings dangled from her ears, nearly brushing her shoulders. One had a feather in it.

It was Lilah. Elizabeth's heart sank when she saw the mischief dancing in her sister's eyes. Lilah was so unpredictable, one never could guess what she was going to say or do.

"Hello, Adam." She flashed Cavanaugh an audacious and dazzling smile. At the familiar use of his first name, several members of his entourage blanched. "I recognize you from your pictures in the newspaper."

Though she would rather undergo oral surgery, the responsibility of making introductions fell to Elizabeth. "Mr. Cavanaugh, this is my sister, Lilah Mason."

"How do you do, Ms. Mason?"

Lilah's shoulder settled against the doorjamb in a relaxed posture that matched her lazy voice and half-mast eyes. "How do I do what?"

One of Cavanaugh's subordinates cleared his throat. Another gasped. From behind Adam's back Elizabeth glared unspoken threats at her sister. But Lilah was undaunted. "If you were on your way out, don't let me keep you."

"I don't intend to." Cavanaugh turned his head and gave Elizabeth a curt nod good-bye, then brushed past Lilah who was still indolently leaning against the doorjamb. The Cavanaugh thanes scurried out in the wake of their angry warlord.

"Lilah, how could you?" Elizabeth hissed as soon as the group had cleared the door.

Lilah laughed easily. "Relax, Elizabeth. You had him eating out of your hand. I was watching through the window. I behaved so badly that you'll seem like an angel by comparison. In essence, I just did you a big favor."

"Well, don't do me any more! You embarrassed me half to death. Mother and Father would be aghast."

Lilah twirled off her shawl with a matador's flourish. "I doubt it. They know I'm the black sheep. Can I have this last chocolate? I didn't think those buzzards were going to leave a single one." She popped the piece of candy in her mouth and chewed with vigor.

Elizabeth rubbed her forehead. "I have a headache."

Lilah took sympathy. "How was it going before I made my entrance? It looked good from where I was standing."

"He's positively charming."

"I could afford to be charming, too, if I had his zillions."

Elizabeth ignored the crack. "I didn't expect him to be so sincere, so human. I thought he'd be brusque and all business. Intimidating."

"Honestly, Lizzie, you take the cake. He's as slick as a billiard ball, but it's all an act. Don't you realize that? Enjoy his charm, but don't fall for it."

"I liked him."

"You're supposed to like him."

"He asked me to meet with him in private sometime soon."

"Oh, really?" Lilah sipped at a cup of tea, made a disagreeable face, and returned it to the table.

"Don't say 'Really?' in that tone of voice. It will be a business meeting." Lilah's expression reeked with skepticism. "*Strictly* business."

"I'm sure it will be." She said it in a tone that indicated she didn't believe it for a minute.

"I don't see why you're so suspicious of him."

"Then I'll tell you why. He's gorgeous, granted. But I'm always leery of men who are that debonaire. I just don't trust them. There's got to be a worm in an apple that shiny."

Elizabeth had tired of the subject. Adam Cavanaugh would probably never speak to her again. He might even terminate her lease after her sister's behavior. "What are you doing here anyway? Don't you have any patients today? And is that the latest in uniforms for physical therapists?"

"That all depends on the kind of therapy one is dispensing," she said with a ribald laugh. "Don't you like the outfit?" Lilah pirouetted and Elizabeth had to admit that her sister looked smashing. "In fact I'm wearing this for one of my patients. He's paraplegic because of a motorcycle accident. He's been bitching that people are prejudiced against bikers, me included. I thought I'd show him just how free-spirited I can be."

Elizabeth's mind backtracked to her conversation with Thad about motorcycles and sitting astride them.

Lilah drew her back to the present. "Written down any fantasies for me?"

"No." Lilah instantly saw through Elizabeth's lie, but before she could take issue with it, a customer entered the store. He looked around uneasily. Elizabeth recognized his symptoms. He was uncomfortable in such a feminine environment, just like a woman would be in a hardware store looking for a particular nut to fit a certain bolt. He was wearing that same lost, bewildered expression. "Can I help you, sir?" she asked him.

"I'm looking for something for my wife. An anniversary gift."

"I have a wide selection of crystal perfume bottles. Would you like to see them?"

Lilah took the brush-off for what it was. She replaced her shawl, then sashayed toward the door. As she went past the nervous man, who was paunchy and balding, she whispered, "Forget the fancy perfume bottles. If you want something that won't collect dust, check out the red satin garter belt."

". . . to the carnival Saturday night."

The last several words of Matt's endless monologue jabbed through Elizabeth's headache and disturbing mental review of her meeting with Adam Cavanaugh. The fork she had been mechanically feeding herself with halted midway between her meat loaf and her mouth. "Carnival?"

"The Fall Festival at school, Mom," Megan patiently explained. She was much like John. He had been a stickler for details. Always organized, on time, and in control. While Elizabeth was unfailingly absent-minded, her daughter never forgot anything.

"Oh, of course. The Fall Festival." She remembered sticking a notice to that effect on the refrigerator door a week or so ago. Glancing toward it now, she saw that the photocopied bulletin had been covered up by a crayon drawing of a grinning jack-o'-lantern and six flying ghosts. "It's this Saturday night?"

"From seven till nine-thirty," Megan informed her. "And we want to stay for the whole time, don't we, Matt?"

"Yeah. The raffle drawing for the compact-disk player isn't until nine-fifteen, so we can't leave before then. Thad said so too."

"Thad? What does he have to do with it?"

"I invited him to go with us."

Elizabeth's fork clattered to her plate. "You didn't really, did you?" she demanded of her son when she was able to speak again.

Matt looked at her warily and nodded his head up and down. "This afternoon."

"And what did he say?" She dreaded to hear.

"He said sure."

Elizabeth rolled her lips inward to keep from uttering the swearwords that surged to mind. "How could you do that, Matt, without consulting me first? I can't believe you did such a thing."

"She said I could."

"Who said you could?"

"My teacher. Miss Blanchard. Both parents are s'pposed to come to the festival. Everybody else has a mom *and* a dad. Since I don't have a dad I asked her if I could 'nvite somebody else and she said I could." His lower lip pooched out and began to tremble. "But you won't let Thad come with us. You won't let us do anything fun. You're mean! You're the meanest mom in the whole world."

In tears, the boy raced from the table, knocking over his glass of milk in the process. Elizabeth let him go. Her head fell forward into her waiting hands. She dismally watched the milk pool on the table, then dribble over the edge onto the tile floor, and still she didn't move.

It had been difficult for Matt when he started public kindergarten and realized that most children had a living father, even if he was divorced from the child's mother and lived in a separate house. Matt had been just a toddler when John was killed, so he didn't remember what it was like to have a father. Elizabeth had spent hours explaining John's death to him. But to a five-year-old child, a deceased father was a difficult concept to grasp, much less become reconciled to.

"Mom, the milk's dripping all over the floor. Do you want me to clean it up?"

Elizabeth raised her head and smoothed her hand over Megan's straight, wheat-colored hair. "No, darling. I'll do it. But thank you for offering."

"I told Matt maybe he should ask you first."

"I'll talk to him when he's had a chance to calm down."

"Are you going to let Thad come with us?"

Her daughter's wistful tone hit Elizabeth like a steamroller. Every little girl needed a daddy and Megan missed having one. "Of course he can come," she heard herself saying as she forced a smile.

After the dishes were done, she went in search of her son and found him sprawled across his bed, his Pooh bear tucked under his arm. Dried tears had left salty tracks on his cheeks. Elizabeth sat down on the edge of the bed and leaned over to kiss his forehead.

"I'm sorry I yelled at you." He said nothing, but swallowed a sob. "I was surprised, that's all." She explained why she should have been consulted before he issued the invitation. "But I guess it's all right this time."

His cloudy eyes cleared immediately. "He can come?"

"If he wants to."

"Gee, that'll be great!"

Yeah, great, Elizabeth thought. After the children were in bed, she reasoned that Thad might be as unenthusiastic about attending the school carnival as she was to have him along. He might have accepted the invitation out of pity for her fatherless children. Shouldn't she give him an opportunity to back out gracefully?

She removed her apron and applied fresh lipstick before walking across the dark lawns. He was sitting in an easy chair on his back porch. Over the weekend he had covered the screens with glass panels to winterize the room. By the light of the TV set, she could see a tray with the remains of his dinner on it. A steak and a beer.

He wasn't watching the television, but reading a magazine. She wondered if it was a men's magazine full of pictures of naked women. If so, now wasn't a good time to come calling. But she'd come this far and she wanted to get this over with as soon as possible so she could stop dreading it. He didn't notice her until she knocked. His head came around and his eyes speared into her like twin lasers.

He left his chair and switched off the TV set before opening the door. He had laid the magazine down in the seat of his chair; Elizabeth didn't have a chance to see the cover.

"Hi," she said awkwardly.

"Hi. Come in."

"No, I, uh, can't stay but a minute. I left the children sleeping." She wasn't about to go into his house alone. What if some of the other neighbors saw her? Human nature being what it was, they would jump to the wrong conclusions. Gossip would spread as quickly as wildfire.

He stepped through the door and reached behind him to close it. "Is something wrong?"

"No. Well, that is, I hope not." She wasn't making any sense and knew he must think she was a jibbering fool. As well as she could remember, she'd never spoken a coherent word to this man. There was no reason for her to be so nervous. He was just a man, for heaven's sake . . . but so *much* man.

"Matt told me he invited you to the Fall Festival at his school," she said in a breathless rush.

"He did."

"Are you going?"

"I told him I would."

"I know. That's what he said. But I don't want you to feel obligated to go just because he asked you to."

He studied her for a moment. "You don't want me along, is that it?"

"No! I mean, yes. I mean . . ." She drew a deep breath. "It's fine with me if you really want to attend something so . . . It's an elementary-school carnival. There'll be a thousand kids running around like wild Indians and frantic parents chasing after them. It's noisy and messy and . . . and . . ." She made a helpless gesture. "It's not something I think you'll enjoy."

"Because I'm a confirmed old bachelor."

Damn! Now I've insulted him, she thought when he turned his back on her and headed toward his Jeep parked in the driveway. "It's not that, Mr. —Thad. I just wanted to give you an opportunity to back out if you wanted to. I'd make it all right with Matt and spare you having to tell him."

He had let down the tailgate of the Jeep and now slid a monstrous box from the back of it. He hefted it to his shoulders and retraced his steps into the backyard. Not knowing what else to do, she dogged his footsteps. He eased the box to the ground.

"I've never had kids, but I'm not so old that I don't remember being one, Elizabeth." When he spoke her name, it did something funny to her tummy. Like his fingers had stroked her there.

"I didn't mean to imply that—"

"I even remember a few school carnivals and how excited I got over them. I was lucky enough to have my mom *and* dad to go with me."

Elizabeth leaned against the nearest tree trunk and sighed. "You make me feel as guilty as Matt did. I scolded him when he told me he had invited you. I was mortified. I didn't want you to feel obligated. He called me the meanest mom in the whole world."

Thad chuckled. "I hardly think you're that. I don't feel obligated to go to the festival. In fact, I think I'll enjoy it a lot. And I didn't want to make you feel guilty. Okay? Now can we stop apologizing? In fact, I'd like to drop the subject altogether. Tell me what you think of this."

He knelt down and tipped the large cardboard box forward. Elizabeth dropped to her knees beside him and studied the photograph on the side of the box.

"A hammock! How lovely."

"You think so?"

"Yes. I've always wanted one. One exactly like this." According to the picture on the box, the hammock was made of woven white jute. Long fringe hung from the sides of it.

"I've always wanted one too. I thought I'd hang it between these two trees." He pointed them out to her.

"Oh, yes. And in the summertime, it'll be wonderful to—" She broke off abruptly.

"To what?" he asked quietly, watching her face. When she declined to answer him, he said, "To lie in?"

"Isn't that what hammocks are for?"

"Uh-huh. Feel free to lie in mine anytime."

"Thank you."

"But you won't, will you?"

She looked up at him quickly, stunned by his keen perception. "Probably not."

"Why not?"

"I wouldn't want to take advantage of the offer."

He shook his head. "Nope. That's not it. You don't want to lie in my hammock because the other neighbors might start gossiping about us. They might think you're lying in my bed as well."

Her stomach bobbed in her middle like a helium balloon, weightless and flighty with nowhere to go. "There's absolutely nothing for the neighbors to gossip about."

"And you're making damn sure it stays that way."

"Do you blame me?"

"Blame?" His brows drew together over the bridge of his nose. " 'Blame' isn't the word I'd use. I just think it's silly for you to go out of your way to avoid me."

She had no comeback so she didn't offer one. He had her pegged and she'd only look sillier to deny his allegation.

"I understand why you go to such lengths," he said softly. "You have to protect your reputation. People are watching to see if you'll slip up, become an irresponsible parent, do something scandalous."

"It's almost a cliché, how young widows are supposed to be— "

"Sex starved," he bluntly supplied. "And I'm a bachelor who lives alone. That in itself makes me suspect. So if you came inside my house for something as innocent as borrowing a cup of sugar, the gossips would have it that we'd had a quickie on the kitchen table." He laughed shortly. "Quickies have their uses, but personally I've never cared much for them. They're like rushing through an excellent bottle of wine. You don't drink it because you're thirsty. You drink it for the pleasure you can derive from its taste." His blue-hot gaze moved to her mouth. "Some things should be savored, lingered over."

Elizabeth's throat had closed to any words she might have uttered, had she been able to think of any. Her heart, however, was making enough racket to compensate. She was certain he could hear it banging against her ribs.

"You're shivering." He raised his hand and touched her arm where the flesh was pebbly.

"I'm cold. I should have brought a sweater with me."

"Come on, I'll walk you to your door."

"That's not necessary."

"It is to me."

They confronted each other stubbornly, but Elizabeth was the one who eventually capitulated. She had left the light on in the kitchen and, as they picked their way across the dark lawns, was amazed to see how much was visible through the windows. She rarely thought to close the blinds because she liked letting the sunlight in during the day.

Could Thad see into her house from his screened back porch? She must remember never to come into the kitchen at night in a state of dishabille or he wouldn't need his girlie magazines to get his kicks.

"Have I thanked you for trimming my side of the hedge?" she asked, remembering that she owed him a thank you.

"Did you notice?"

"I noticed. Thanks. How are the puppies?"

"Doing very well. Growing."

"Good." They had reached her back door and could, thankfully, end this ridiculous conversation.

"What time Saturday?" he asked.

"I think the kids said seven. If you're sure."

"I'm sure. I'll pick you up."

She started to object, but something in the determined set of his chin prevented that. "Okay. That sounds fine, Thad. Well, good night."

"Elizabeth." He caught her hand before she could shield herself with the screen door.

"Yes?"

"Have they healed?" He ran his thumb over the palm of her hand. His touch was feather-light, but it might just as well have been electric for the currents it sent through her arm.

"My hands? Yes. They've healed. Completely."

As though doubting her, he raised her hand closer to his face and studied the palm. He was still staring at it when he said, "If you should ever need me, for any reason, call. To hell with what the neighbors think."

When he did lift his gaze back to hers, it took her breath. Before she could regain enough of it to offer a comment or another good night, he released her hand and disappeared in the darkness.

Four

The stranger emerged from the darkness. He was spawned from it and was one with it. He materialized in front of me—tall, wide of shoulder, narrow of hip, a delta-shaped torso of manly muscle.

I couldn't see his face clearly, but I knew him instantly. His features were indistinct, but I recognized him. And because I did, his sudden appearance wasn't frightening. Exciting, yes. Thrilling, definitely. Forbidden, by all means. But not frightening.

He said nothing. Nor did I. Words were superfluous. We knew what the other expected, wanted. In the darkness we would give and take without inhibition. Pleasure was our common ground. Personalities were made insignificant by primal need. Neither pasts nor futures mattered. Only this present. This present redolent with a carnality which must be admitted, addressed, and assuaged to our mutual satisfaction.

He reached out and stroked my hair. Slowly he removed the single pin which magically held it all up. It spilled luxuriantly over and through his fingers. I knew this pleased him, that he loved the feel of my hair in his hands. Even though I still couldn't distinguish his face, I knew he was smiling as he slid his fingers through the thick strands.

I laid my hands on his chest. Strangely, I wasn't shy. In this velvet-dark realm, timidity didn't exist. Boldness was expected, even invited. No one would see. No one would know. The darkness was a friendly entity. It cloaked every indiscretion and made all things acceptable. Here one wouldn't be held accountable for his actions. There were no rules of behavior, no duties beyond satisfying every secret lust.

The hard, muscled curves of his chest filled my palms. I curled my fingers into the firm flesh that barely yielded to the pressure. He was wearing a shirt, but merely a thought from me dissolved it and his chest was instantly bare.

Inquisitively I combed through the pelt of springy hair. My fingertips were sensitized to each nuance of texture and form. His nipples were hard and distended, like pebbles. I leaned forward and made one wet with the tip of my tongue. He moaned with pleasure.

He cradled my face between his hands and tilted it up. He stroked my damp lips with his thumbs. Parting them, he ran the pads of his thumbs over my teeth. I bit him lightly, playfully scraping my teeth against his skin.

He slid his hands down my neck, then farther down my chest to my breasts. Taking them in his hands, he kneaded them gently, rubbing the nipples with his fingertips until they peaked.

Our lips came together in a fiery kiss. A fierce melding of mouths. His tongue mated with mine.

Passions flared. Roughly he backed me against a wall that I hadn't known was there. He could barely control this savage hunger that had suddenly seized him. I found it exhilarating and trembled in response to it.

He kissed his way down my throat, then his hot, seeking mouth closed around my nipple. Its ardent tugging motion coaxed an involuntary moan from my lips. Instinctually, I knew that his eyes were closed, that he was indulging an unspoken need within himself. I wanted to have milk to feed him with, and, when I said those words aloud, he was deeply touched.

His hands contracted in a gentle love-squeeze at my waist before moving over my hipbones. All I need do was ask, and my greatest desire would be fulfilled. That I knew. But I said nothing. I wanted to prolong the delicious agony of escalating desire. Besides, requests were unnecessary. Unselfishly he anticipated my needs. All I had to do was think of what I wanted and he would do it.

He knew precisely when and how to enter me. The taking was sudden, swift, sure. He filled my yearning body with his steely heat. It stroked me to the brink of oblivion. His hands were everywhere, gliding over my skin. His mouth was everywhere, open and hot.

He exercised no discipline. He had no conscience. He'd been bred to give pleasure. Born of sexual desire, suckled on lust, he knew nothing else but to give me ultimate joy and satisfaction. The fury of my orgasm was beyond anything I'd ever experienced before or had known was possible.

Totally spent, damp with my sweat, with his, I clung to him weakly. Tenderly and affectionately, he stroked my hair, lifting it off my dewy shoulders. At last, his features still obscured by the forgiving and redeeming darkness, he left me and receded into the nothingness from which he had come.

I had never seen my incredible lover's face. Never heard his voice. Yet I would know him should he ever come to me again.

The incessant buzzing inside her head didn't recede with her faceless lover. It stayed in her bloodstream like a pain-killing narcotic long after the pain was gone.

Groggy and disoriented, Elizabeth came awake and opened her eyes. Lord, but she felt drained. Her four limbs weighed a ton apiece. A complacent smile lingered on her moist lips. She couldn't scoop together an ounce of energy. Lassitude held her anchored to the bed and incapable of movement. Her skin was covered with a sheen of perspiration. Her nightgown was hopelessly twisted and clinging to her. A provocative heat resided between her thighs. It was concentrated there, having been funneled there from her entire system. Her nipples were stiff. They tingled.

Suddenly she blinked, realizing that the buzzing inside her head wasn't the aftereffect of incredibly erotic lovemaking but the drone of a power chain saw coming from somewhere in the neighborhood. There was no lover, mysterious or otherwise. She lay alone in her chaste bed. It wasn't dark. Sunlight was streaming through her shuttered windows.

The day was Saturday. And later this day, she had a date with Thad Randolph.

Heaving a sigh of dread, she swung her feet to the floor and sat up on the edge of the bed. The clock on her nightstand told her it was a few minutes after nine. She reached for her robe lying across the end of the bed and pulled it on, overlapping it across her breasts, pretending that their crests weren't still itchy and flushed. She stood up, trying to support herself on legs that were wobbly and weak.

"Lilah would have loved that one," she mumbled as she padded into the bathroom. Talk about fantasies! Lord! The ol' nameless, faceless, voiceless, guiltless encounter couldn't be topped for sheer eroticism. It was every woman's most secret fantasy because everything was permissible. There were no consequences to deal with later.

Sick—that's what she was. If the state authorities knew what she had dreamed about, they'd probably take her children away from her.

After taking a shower, a very cold one, she found her children in the kitchen eating bowls of presweetened cereal. She'd let sugar win the war over natural fiber years ago, having decided that the final victory wouldn't be worth the morning battles. She kissed and hugged her children in turn before starting the coffeemaker.

"Tonight's the night of the carnival, Mom," Matt reminded her through a mouthful of empty calories and pastel, teeth-rotting goo.

"That's right."

She tried to interject enthusiasm into her voice. All week, she'd avoided thinking about this Saturday night, as if thinking about it would attach some special significance to it.

She hadn't seen Thad since he'd walked her to her back door Monday evening. The children had given her daily progress reports on Penny's puppies, but she hadn't solicited any information about Thad. It was almost a relief that the dreaded day had finally arrived. By this time tomorrow, it would be over and done with.

"Don't be late getting home. Thad said he'd be

here a few minutes before seven to pick us up," Megan told her.

"I promise not to be late," Elizabeth said a little too sharply. She modified her tone and said, "I'll get here in plenty of time to change. Just be sure that all your chores are done. I'm leaving a list for Mrs. Alder."

Ordinarily on Saturdays the hours she spent in Fantasy crawled by. She was guiltily aware that her children were out of school and spending a great part of their weekend at home without her. But this Saturday, the time flew. She couldn't retard the hours' rapid march no matter how many menial tasks she masochistically assigned herself. Five o'clock arrived. She locked up and drove home.

The children were so excited they nearly tackled her when she came through the door. "Thad called and said he'd be here at six forty-five. *Hurry*, Mom."

"Megan, that's an hour and a half away. I'll be ready. I promise."

But of course she wasn't.

Baby threw up something that looked like pimento cheese on the living-room sofa. It had to be cleaned up immediately. Matt and Megan got in a scuffle over the remote control of the TV. That resulted in Matt banging his head on the corner of the coffee table hard enough to break the skin. He bled on his hair and the carpet. Both had to be washed.

Elizabeth broke a nail on her bureau drawer. When she tried to repair it, she super-glued two fingers together. By the time she got around to eye makeup, she was so rushed and nervous she couldn't get it right. She couldn't decide what to wear. So she was standing in her bare feet and underwear when Matt came into her bedroom at six forty-three to see if she was ready.

"Aw, Mom!" he wailed when he saw that she wasn't.

She was as incredulous over his appearance as he was over hers. He was wearing clothing fit only for a ragpicker. "Matthew, those jeans have holes in the knees. Go put on your new ones."

"They're all stiff and scratchy."

"They are not. I washed and dried them twice." Standing at her closet door, she wondered if she should wear her blue chambray skirt or the black slacks fresh from the cleaners?

"I want to wear these jeans. They're cool."

The blue chambray skirt. "Your new ones, please, sir. And that sweatshirt is big enough for me. Go change right now. Put on your green polo shirt."

"It's dorky."

"You're not going out in public—"

The doorbell pealed. "He's here!" Matt screeched.

"Come back here!" Elizabeth called. But she could already hear her son clumping down the stairs trying to beat his sister to the front door.

"I'll get it!"

"I'll get it!"

Elizabeth never knew which one made it to the door first. The next voice she heard was Thad's. "Hi. I see you're ready and raring to go."

"We are," Megan told him.

"But Mom's not," Matt was overheard to say. "She's always late 'cause she lies in the bathtub till all the bubbles are gone. She's putting on her clothes. Sometimes that takes a long time too."

"Well, we're not in that big a hurry, are we? Why don't we wait for her in the living room?"

Upstairs, Elizabeth happened to catch a glimpse of herself in the cheval glass that stood in the corner of her bedroom. She had an ear pressed to her door so as not to miss a single word and had her long skirt clutched to her chest.

Impatient with herself for looking and acting ridiculous, even to herself, she stepped into the skirt and pulled a soft white wool sweater over her head. She gathered her hair back into a ponytail, quickly misted herself with fragrance, and left the room.

She didn't want Thad Randolph to think she was primping for him like a coed keeping her prom date waiting. She took the stairs with an aggressive tread, but paused before entering the living room. He was standing with his back to her, listening while Matt explained the intricacies of a Legos battleship he was building.

"Hello."

At the sound of her voice, he came around on the heels of his boots. Dressed in jeans, a plain cotton sports shirt, and a gray suede bomber jacket that did terrific things for his hair and eyes, he made an impressive escort. Slightly better than impressive. He made her palms sweat.

"Hi. Matt said you were still getting dressed." His eyes swept down her body, all the way to the toes of her ivory leather boots with the slouch cuff, then back up again. "I hope we didn't rush you."

"No. Are we ready?" He nodded. The children exuberantly chorsued their readiness.

Matt delayed them by putting up an argument against taking a jacket. Elizabeth insisted on it, since many of the festival's activities were outdoors. And a jacket would camouflage his choice of wardrobe.

"The sooner you get your jacket, the sooner we can leave," Thad remarked.

Matt made it upstairs to his room and back in record time. Thad escorted them out. He was flanked by Matt and Megan. Elizabeth brought up the rear after locking the door behind them. It felt strange to be riding in the front seat of Thad's Jeep wagon with him behind the wheel and the children in the back seat. To anyone observing them, they would look like the all-American family on an outing. The thought made her jittery.

So much so that she actually jumped when Thad said, "You look pretty tonight."

He had wedged the unexpected compliment in sideways between her children's nonstop chatter. "Thank you. So do you. Look nice, I mean."

"Thanks."

They smiled across the front seat at each other. Elizabeth's insides quivered slightly beneath his appreciative blue gaze. She was actually grateful to Matt when he demanded Thad's attention.

The school building was almost rocking with the activity going on inside it. The campus was swarming with hyper children and their parents, who tried in vain to keep up with them as they raced from one gaily decorated booth to another, plying their skills at the various games.

The first order of business was to purchase tickets that were redeemable at all the booths and concession stands. Elizabeth knew the PTA officer who was selling them and had no choice but to introduce her to Thad. So avid was the other woman's curiosity that she miscounted his change twice before giving him the correct amount.

"You should have let me buy the tickets," Elizabeth told him as they moved away from the ticket booth. She was aware of every curious glance and whispering tongue.

"Consider it my contribution to the local PTA," he replied, unperturbed. "Where to first, kids?"

Elizabeth's fears that he would have an awful time

were unfounded. To her surprise Thad got into the spirit of the festival. He offered Megan advice at the Fishin' Hole and she ended up winning a bottle of liquid bubbles. At the basketball goal, he held Matt up so he'd have a better chance at scoring. Matt came away from that with a bag of marbles in his hand and a grin on his face that made Elizabeth's heart ache. She saw the smug glances her son cast his friends as he walked away with Thad. He didn't have a father to brag to the other boys about and was taking full advantage of Thad's prowess.

They stopped at several other booths before Elizabeth asked, "Is anybody hungry? It's either spaghetti or hot dogs," she informed their guest apologetically.

"Great. I'm starved."

They decided on hot dogs. Matt and Megan ate theirs in about three bites. "Can we get our faces painted, Mom?" Megan asked after slurping up the last of her soft drink.

Matt was hopping up and down beside his chair. "Yeah, I want to get the devil face."

"How appropriate." Elizabeth laughed, pinching him on his mustard-smeared cheek.

"Can we, Mom? It only costs six tickets."

"Thad and I haven't eaten yet."

"That'll take forever." Megan moaned. "Then you'll want to drink coffee for an hour."

"Would it be all right if they went alone?" Thad asked her.

"Can we, Mom? Can we?"

"*May* we," she corrected. "Yes, you may if you promise to come right back here. If you get lost in this crowd, we'll never find you. And stay together," she called after them.

Clutching the tickets Thad had doled out to them,

they squirmed their way through the cafeteria crowd and out into the jammed corridor toward the face-painting booth.

"Oh, to have that much energy," Thad said, taking the first bite out of his hot dog.

Elizabeth shook her head remorsefully. "I tried to warn you. You'll be exhausted by the time you get home tonight."

"I'm having a great time."

The wonder of it was that he truly seemed to be enjoying himself. He was as interested in the school as the PTA mothers were in Elizabeth Burke's "date." As though reading her mind, he said, "I'm an oddity, aren't I? Or am I getting paranoid? Is everyone staring at me, or is that my imagination?"

She smiled and ducked her head shyly. "They're staring. Everybody knows I'm single."

"How long have you been single? When was your husband killed?" She glanced up at him in surprise. "One of the neighbors told me when I moved in," he replied to her unspoken question. "I didn't ask. The information was volunteered."

Because he seemed so sincere, she didn't find it awkward to share with him the facts surrounding her husband's death. "John was killed two years ago. Automobile accident. He was pronounced dead at the scene."

"Were you and the children with him?"

"No."

"Thank God."

"It happened on his way to work. Two policemen came to the house that morning and asked me to go to the hospital with them." She returned her half-eaten hot dog to the paper plate. "I was changing the shelf paper in the kitchen cabinets. I'll never forget that. When I got home that afternoon, all the dishes were still stacked on the table and the cupboard doors were standing open. For a minute, I couldn't remember why."

"A sudden death like that, it must have been rough on you."

"It was like having the world pulled out from under me." Willfully shaking off her reflective mood, she looked at him. "Have you ever lost anyone close to you?"

"No. Not that way," he said shortly. "Would you like some coffee?"

"Please."

He left the table and headed for the booth where beverages were being dispensed. Elizabeth watched as he made halting progress through the crowd. He had lost someone, but not by death. Who? How? Had he been rejected by someone he loved?

Heads turned; eyes followed him. He captured the attention of nearly every woman his shadow fell on. What woman wouldn't be attracted? Physically, he had a rugged, hard-hat appeal. But his personality was incongruous with his physique. He was sensitive and soft-spoken. He wasn't out to prove how macho he was. His masculinity spoke for itself.

She had never seen a woman at his house, but it was obvious that he didn't live like a monk. He had perfected a method of being sexy and courteous at the same time. He knew how to treat a woman like a lady. And he knew how to treat a lady like a woman.

He wasn't an octopus with groping hands, but he didn't shy away from taking her elbow and guiding her through a crowd. Several times she'd felt his hand at the small of her back, giving her a gentle nudge forward. These mannerly touches had never failed to elicit a thrill.

No, around a woman, he wasn't awkward at all.

Why, then, was he single? Had he had a disastrous marriage and messy divorce that turned him off marriage forever? Did monthly alimony payments make a second marriage economically unfeasible? Or did he simply enjoy the sexual freedom of a bachelor's life? Why *hadn't* she seen any women around his house?

He set the Styrofoam cup of coffee in front of her. "Cream or sugar?"

"Sugar." He passed her a packet of sugar which he'd had the foresight to bring back to the table with him. She absently opened the packet and stirred the sugar into her cup with a plastic spoon. "Have you ever been married, Thad?"

"No." He sipped his coffee, staring at her through the rising steam.

"Oh." She had hoped for some elaboration, but apparently his private life was just that.

"I'm straight, if that's what you're wondering."

She burned her tongue on her coffee. Embarrassment stained her throat and face with vivid color. "I wasn't."

"Sure you were."

She couldn't quite meet that teasing gaze. "Maybe I was. Subconsciously."

"No offense taken. Unfortunately, if I had set out to prove to you that I am heterosexual, you would have been offended." Mischief turned his eyes an even deeper shade of blue. "Although I'd be more than happy to accommodate you if you want proof."

Her previous blush was mild compared to the one that suffused her now. "I believe you." She cleared her throat. "It's just that by the time a man gets to be your age, he's usually been married at least once."

"By the time a man gets to be my age, he's done just about everything at least once," he said, teasing her again. He smiled with her, then lowered his head and stared into his coffee. "I've had several opportunities to get married. There have been a few serious involvements that could have eventually led to marriage, I suppose, but none of them worked out before one or both of us lost interest." Lifting his head, he asked, "Why haven't you remarried?"

Her mind had latched on to his "serious involvements," so it was a moment before she assimilated his question. "I was very much in love with John. We had a good marriage. For a long time after he died, I was in an emotional vacuum. Then I got busy with Fantasy. You know what it takes for anybody to run a business single-handed. The problems are quadrupled if you're a widow with children. I had to be both parents to them. All that combined didn't leave much time and energy for a personal life. And," she said, drawing a deep breath, "I haven't fallen in love with anyone else."

"I guess that's the bottom line, isn't it?"

"Are you saying you've never been in love?"

"In lust, maybe. I've met a lot of women I liked sleeping with, but damned few I enjoyed waking up with." Even over the crowd's noise, Elizabeth heard his quietly spoken afterthought. "Maybe that'll be the determining factor. I'll know I'm in love when it's that woman I want to wake up with every morning."

For a moment their eyes locked and held. It was Matt's voice that finally broke the compelling stare. "Hey, look, Thad."

The boy's face was a mask of red and black paint, broken only by his wide, gap-toothed grin. Megan had had her face done like a pierrette doll with eloquently tearful eyes and a red heart for a mouth.

"Megan, you look great!" Thad exclaimed. "But where the *devil* is Matt?"

The boy lapsed into a fit of giggles and cannoned into Thad's chest. When the hilarity had died down, Megan asked, "Have you finished your coffee yet?"

Thad glanced at Elizabeth and shrugged helplessly. "Yes, we're finished," he told the impatient children. He helped Elizabeth out of her chair. Bending his head close to hers in order to make himself heard, he said, "Should we take in the outdoor events?"

"I suppose so. If for no other reason than to justify Matt having to bring his jacket."

Laughing, Thad put his arm across her shoulders and gave her a quick hug. The gesture was friendly, not seductive. There was no reason for her heart to skip several beats. None whatsoever. A man didn't mention the women he slept with to one he wanted to take to bed. He discussed past affairs with a buddy, a pal. If this relationship developed into anything, that's the direction it would take. They would be friends, not lovers.

But apparently Thad didn't know that. "Careful," he said when she stumbled on uneven pavement in the playground. He slid his fingers between hers and linked their hands. Her arm became sandwiched between his arm and his side. His elbow pressed an indentation at least an inch deep into her breast. Occasionally, and she was certain accidentally, the back of his arm grazed her nipple. Its invariable response shot to hell the palsy-walsy theory.

"Can we go on the hayride, Mom?"

"Sure." Her voice was reedy and thin.

The two children scrambled aboard the horse-drawn wagon. The driver said, "Sorry, but I can't take responsibility for the kids unless at least one parent goes too."

"No problem," Thad said. "We were going anyway."

He stepped up into the wagon and extended a

hand down to Elizabeth. She had lost control of the situation and couldn't quite decide when or how it had happened. The people already sitting in the wagon and all those standing in line behind her were watching her expectantly. Her choices were to create an unpleasant scene, or to grasp Thad's hand and let him pull her up beside him. Taking the easy way out, she opted for the latter.

Thad made certain that Matt and Megan were safely sitting down before finding Elizabeth and him a spot in the hay. She tucked her skirt around her legs, careful not to rub thighs with him.

"Isn't this fun, Mom?" Megan asked over the heads of those people sitting between them. All eyes swung in Elizabeth's direction.

"It's a blast," she answered, forcing a smile. She was aware of Thad's arm resting on the slats of the wagon behind her. If she leaned back, even a fraction of an inch, she'd be within the curve of his arm. She'd never kept such rigid posture.

The man operating the hayride maximized the capacity of the wagon. As he loaded the last waiting group, he said, "Scrunch up, please, so everybody can get on. Ma'am, if you wouldn't mind sitting in your husband's lap, it'll make more room."

With horror, Elizabeth realized that he was speaking to her. She remained as still as a wooden Indian. Everybody in the wagon turned to glare at the uncooperative spoilsport who was holding up the proceedings.

"Elizabeth?"

She heard Thad's soft inquiry, like a caressing breath on her ear, but she didn't look at him. Instead, feeling helpless and resigned, she offered no resistance when he lifted her onto his lap.

"Thanks." The driver of the wagon closed the tailgate behind the last passengers. He moved to the front, took his seat on the top of the wagon, and picked up the reins. Flicking the horse's rump with them, he called back, "Hold on, folks. Here we go."

The wagon lurched forward. Because she was sitting so stiff and straight, Elizabeth was thrown off balance. She landed hard against Thad's chest. Her bottom slipped into the notch of his thighs. She heard him grunt softly and wondered if it was from pleasure or pain, unsure which she would rather it be.

"Did you hear what that man said, Mom?" Megan called out to her. "He thought Thad was your husband."

"That'd be neat," the devil with the red and black face chimed in. "Then I'd have a real dad instead of one who just lives in heaven."

Groaning, Elizabeth closed her eyes and prayed for invisibility. She blessed the merciful soul who started a round of "Row, Row, Row Your Boat" and drew the crowd's attention away from her.

She felt the vibration of Thad's silent laughter through his gray suede jacket. "Remind me to murder my children later," she muttered. "I'm so sorry, Thad."

"For what?"

"For embarrassing you."

"You're the one who's embarrassed, not me."

"And for having to sit on your lap. I hope you don't mind too much."

His eyes held hers. "Not at all. In fact, as long as we're here," he added gruffly as he slipped his arms around her, "we'd just as well relax and enjoy the, uh . . . ride."

•   •   •

He had been charming. His manners had been flawless. He could have been a real cad about having her sit on his lap during the hayride. He could have taken unfair advantage of the situation and sneaked a feel in the dark. It would have been easy, considering that his hands were clasped together just below her breasts for the duration of the jostling ride. But he hadn't.

He'd been a perfect gentleman. Hadn't he offered her his jacket when the night air had grown cold? Yes, he had. That's when she'd felt his warm breath feather her neck. That's when she'd been tempted to relax her rigid posture, to let her neck go limp, and to rest her head on his shoulder. But she could hardly initiate something romantic when he'd gone out of his way to keep things platonic, could she?

He'd maintained that friendly, gentlemanly attitude all evening. He had commiserated with Megan and Matt when their raffle tickets for the compact-disk player turned out to be losers. He had thanked them repeatedly for inviting him to the Fall Festival. He hadn't dropped them at the curb, but walked them up the sidewalk to their front door and saw them safely inside. His smile had been open and companionable with nary a trace of suggestiveness when he said a private good night to Elizabeth and thanked her again for letting him go with them.

He had been a good sport about the whole thing.

So, dammit, why was she disappointed?

At home now, alone in her upstairs bedroom with the lamp turned low and the shutters closed, why did she wish he'd done something just a shade shady?

He could have given her one soft nuzzle on the neck during the hayride. He could have raked his thumb along the undersides of her breasts just to let her know that he knew they were there and that they weren't bad for a close-to-thirty mother of two.

When he helped her down from the wagon, he could have held her against him a second or two longer. When he told her good night after the children had already been sent upstairs to get ready for bed, he could have invited himself in for a quick cup of coffee. He could have given her a friendly good-night kiss on the cheek. He could have done *something* a little less nice and a lot more exciting.

Not that she wanted anything of a romantic nature to spark between them. She didn't. It was just that it had been a far more pleasant evening than she'd had any right to expect. He was even more attractive than she had originally thought. His past affairs intrigued her and she was mad to know what kind of woman appealed to him. A man like him didn't stay celibate for long stretches of time. He was a gentleman, but he wasn't dead, and every time that wagon had found a dip in the soccer field and her hips had ground against his lap . . . No, he definitely wasn't dead.

Oh, hell. She was being ridiculous. Vexed by her own silliness, she switched off the lamp and pulled the covers up to her chin. Irrationally she was furious with him for being so nice.

Five

She was still furious when she drove to the market
the following afternoon. Since she wasn't going far
and wouldn't be gone long, she had left Megan and
Matt at home to do their weekend homework. Shopping without them was always easier than having
them along, pestering her to buy things they didn't
need and couldn't afford.

The aisles of the supermarket were virtually deserted since the Chicago Bears game was being tele-
vised that afternoon. She located everything on her
list quickly and was heading for the checkout lane
when she saw him enter the store. If he hadn't
spotted her at the same time, she would have made
a point to avoid him.

As it was, she gave him a vapid smile and a brief
nod, wheeled her basket one hundred and eighty
degrees, and took off in the opposite direction. Thinking that she had adroitly maneuvered herself out of
an unwelcome encounter, she drew up short when
he rounded the end of the next aisle and they met
face-to-face.

"Hi."

"Hi, Thad."

"You've got quite a basketful."

"A whole week's worth. I try to get all my grocery shopping done on the weekend. The week gets so busy. But it seems like I always forget something. As often as not I end up stopping at the store at least once a day anyway." She let her inane chatter dwindle and die. Nervously she shifted from one sneaker-shod foot to the other. "I thought you'd be watching the ball game like every other conscientious fan."

His lips quirked in a smile. "It's halftime. I came out for reinforcements." He held up a bag of potato chips and a six-pack of beer.

"Oh, well, don't let me keep you." She rolled her basket forward.

"If you've got everything, I'll follow you home and carry your groceries in for you."

"No!" Her exclamation took them both by surprise. "I mean, I wouldn't hear of keeping you from the ball game."

"No problem, the Bears are ahead by twenty-one points. It's boring."

Before she could stop him, he added his potato chips and beer to her shopping cart, moved her aside, and assumed command of it the way the captain of a ship relieves his boatswain of the wheel.

"Really, Thad, there's no need—"

"Well, hello!"

Thad had taken the blind turn at the end of the aisle and crashed into the cart being pushed by the room mother of Megan's class.

"Hi," Elizabeth said sickly.

"I saw you at the festival last night. Did you enjoy it?" Her eyes were snapping back and forth between the two of them.

"I had a great time," Thad replied, since the question had obviously been directed toward him.

"How nice. They can be such fun." No one said anything for several seconds. "Well, see you."

"See you." Elizabeth knew that it would circulate through the membership of the PTA that she was more than a casual acquaintance with her date to the Fall Festival. They had been seen shopping together on a Sunday afternoon. That implied . . . Well, one's imagination could run rampant.

She waited for the woman to move out of earshot, then took the chips and beer out of her cart and shoved them back at Thad. "I just remembered something else I need to get. Thanks for the offer to carry in my groceries, but you'd better get home. I'm sure halftime is over by now. Bye."

She was off before he had time to argue. Since the room mother had headed for the dairy case, Elizabeth picked the produce section on the opposite side of the store. She'd browse there until Thad had had sufficient time to leave.

"What gives?"

Elizabeth dropped the orange she'd been squeezing and spun around. Thad was standing only inches from her, a grocery bag propped on his hip. It was the first time she'd ever seen him in an angry mood. His brows were lowered into a near scowl.

"I don't know what you mean."

"Why'd you give me the classic brush-off?"

"I didn't."

"Didn't you?"

"No. I—I remembered that I promised the kids a pumpkin to carve a jack-o'-lantern out of." He glanced down at the orange bin, trapping her in her lie. "I just hadn't gotten around to them yet," she said defensively.

She deserted the oranges and pushed her basket toward the display of colorful pumpkins. Halloween was still a couple of weeks away. Any jack-o'-lantern carved out now would be furry with mold and wrinkled with old age by then, but she had to give her lie validity.

Every pumpkin in the pyramid-shaped display received her careful scrutiny. Thad was subjecting her to just as careful a scrutiny. She was glad she was wearing the old pink knit sweat suit. Dressed this unglamorously, she hardly looked like a widow trying to entice her bachelor neighbor.

He was dressed just as casually as she, but still managed to look attractive in a rumpled, comfy, Sunday-afternoon way. He was wearing jeans that were almost bleached white, run-down deck shoes without socks, and a sweatshirt so old that the university seal on the front had bleached to indecipherability.

He looked like he'd just gotten out of bed and pulled on the first available clothing at hand. Why that should be such a sexy thought, Elizabeth couldn't imagine. Except that she could see it happening . . . with her lying in bed watching as he stepped into the snug jeans and zipped them.

She didn't want to notice anything about him. Not the way he was dressed, or the way he smelled, or the way his hair was endearingly uncombed. Unreasonable as it was, she was miffed at him for not making a pass at her last night. He'd had several golden opportunities, but had capitalized on none of them. Of course, she would have turned him down flat, but he could have *tried*. Was she that undesirable? That unappealing?

She'd awakened that morning to the nameless-lover fantasy again. Only this time, the lover's features had been disturbingly similar to the man who was now studying her with remarkable blue eyes as though trying to figure her out.

"Picked one yet?" he asked.

"Which one do you like best?"

"I like the chubby ones."

"So do I. What do you think of that one?" She pointed at a fat pumpkin.

"Looks good."

"I'll send the bag boy over for it then."

"I'll carry it."

"Really, Thad, don't bother. You're missing your ball game."

He looked hard at her for a moment before relenting. "Okay. Maybe later tonight I can come over and help you carve it out."

"I can manage, but thanks."

"These things can be tricky. One slip of the butcher knife— "

"I'm perfectly capable of carving a Halloween jack-o'-lantern for my children."

Her tone was just plain bitchy. His scowl told her he didn't like it a bit. She had guessed he wouldn't back down from a fight and she was right. He set his grocery bag on the bin of Golden Delicious apples and leaned forward, putting his face to within inches of hers.

"All right, forget the carving, forget the pumpkin, forget the groceries. Let's talk about something else. What bee got up your butt since last night?"

Her jaw went slack and she took a step backward. His deliberate vulgarity shocked her. "I don't know what you mean," she said, lying.

"The hell you don't. What happened between last night and this afternoon to make me persona non grata?"

"Nothing."

"That's what I thought. So why aren't we friends anymore? Was it that broad we just ran into? Did you let her curiosity get to you? Are you afraid of the gossip that'll circulate if we're seen together?" He ran a hand through his sexily mussed hair. "Look, Elizabeth, they're going to talk about you simply because you're a young widow with a pretty face and a great body. They'll gossip about us whether we ever go to bed together or not."

"Which we won't!"

His eyes narrowed. With one vicious swipe of his arm, he picked up his sack of groceries. Golden Delicious apples went tumbling over the edge of the bin to the floor. "You've got that right. Chameleons are just lizards as far as I'm concerned. They give me the creeps."

"He's gonna get all mushy by Halloween."

"Then we'll carve another one," Elizabeth told her dubious children.

"Why did you put him in the back window, Mom?"

"Don't you think he looks good there?"

"Yeah, but nobody can see him but us."

Us and the neighbor who lives behind us, Elizabeth was thinking. That's why she'd put the largest candle possible in the pumpkin shell before placing the sneering jack-o'-lantern in the kitchen window. The fact that the neighbor's house was dark and his Jeep wasn't parked in the driveway took a little gilt off her triumph. That and the fact that one of the jack-o'-lantern's eyeballs had been cut out when the butcher knife slipped. She'd had to secure it back in place with toothpicks, but that wouldn't be noticeable from Thad's screened porch.

"He's for our enjoyment," she said with a bright, brittle parody of a smile. "When he gets yucky, I'll buy another pumpkin and we'll carve him too. Now, help me clean up this mess."

"Can we toast the seeds?"

"Not tonight. It's bedtime."

It was an hour later before bedtime became official and the children were tucked in, prayers said, last drinks of water gotten, final trips to the john taken. Thad, she was dismayed to hear, had been added to each child's list of God blesses along with her, Daddy in heaven, Aunt Lilah, and Grandma and Grandpa from each side of the family. Depending on their behavior any given day, Mrs. Alder's inclusion was optional. She wondered if Thad would become a permanent fixture on those lists.

His Jeep still wasn't in his driveway when she blew out the candle in the jack-o'-lantern and went upstairs to bed. She read for a while, trying to get sleepy, but she couldn't concentrate on the tedious plot of her library novel.

How dare he talk to her like that? "What bee got up your butt since last night?" What was she supposed to have done when he walked into the grocery store? Act all aflutter? Lower her eyelashes demurely and humbly thank him for accompanying her and her children to the Fall Festival?

And he had called *her* a chameleon! One second he'd been mild-mannered Clark Kent and the next he'd been a vulgar-talking heel with a wounded ego. She would be better off to nip this blooming friendship in the bud. He was too volatile. Actually she knew very little about him. Now she didn't want to. Things should have stayed the way they had been before the day Baby got trapped in the tree. Mr. Thad Randolph had been a distant neighbor, somewhat of a mystery man. She wished he had remained so.

She didn't turn out her lamp until she heard his Jeep pulling into his driveway. Convincing herself that the sleepiness that suddenly overtook her was a coincidence, she snuggled beneath the covers.

But moments later, she threw them off, swearing beneath her breath. She remembered that she'd left the lawn sprinkler on. She'd turned it on early that afternoon and it had been running ever since. Great for the water bill, she thought as she padded through the dark house, down the stairs, and across the kitchen to the back door.

The concrete porch was cold on her bare feet. The night air made her shiver because she hadn't taken time to pull on a robe over her nightgown. Holding up the hem of her long nightgown so it wouldn't trail in the wet grass, she tiptoed toward the water hydrant built into the foundation of the house. It took her a moment to find it in the darkness, but she finally did, and, bending at the waist, turned it off. She gave it one final twist to make certain it was completely shut off before she straightened up and turned around.

The gasp of surprise froze in her throat. She flattened her hand against her chest to still her drumming heartbeat. Then she recognized the form emerging from the impenetrable shadows as Thad Randolph. His features were obscured by the darkness, but the moonlight shining on his hair and turning it silver made him immediately identifiable.

She didn't blurt out the question "What are you doing here?" because she already knew. She didn't know how she knew; she just knew.

She wasn't surprised and therefore didn't flinch when he raised his hand and took a strand of her hair between his fingers. He rubbed it slowly, letting it sift through his fingers sensuously. Then he closed his hand around her throat, and, as though the warmth of his fingers melted the vetebrae in her neck, her head obligingly tipped to one side.

He pressed his lips against that vulnerable curve, giving it a long kiss. Then, gazing down into her face, he touched her lips with his thumb and traced their shape. Responding to his touch, her lips became so pliant they parted slightly. He ran the pad of his thumb over her teeth.

Emboldened, she laid her hands on his chest. Moving aside his unbuttoned shirt, she caressed bare skin, crisp hair, his nipples.

He made a hissing sound and, with one sudden movement, lightly slammed her back into the wall of the house. She saw his head descending toward hers. Her eyes slid closed a second before his lips covered hers. He tilted his head, adjusted the angle, then sank his tongue into the heat of her mouth.

Elizabeth slumped bonelessly, glad that the wall was there to help support her while she surrendered to Thad's mastery and expertise. She'd never been kissed this thoroughly. Never. Even in her fantasies. His kiss seemed to draw the very life out of her and yet at the same time to imbue her with new fire.

His tongue plumbed her mouth with sleek thrusts that suspended her breathing. Then he imbedded it snugly inside and stroked the roof of her mouth. Her body and heart and soul exploded. Splinters of light scattered through her.

His mouth gently ate its way down her neck. His tongue playfully batted against her earlobe before his teeth clamped down on it in a love bite. He kissed her throat, her chest, his mouth open and hot and hungry. When it closed around her nipple, her back reflexively arched and all ten of her fingers clutched his hair. He drew the ripe tip into his mouth, nightgown and all, and sucked it with passionate need.

Clasping her around the waist, he held her steady and in place while he angled his hips forward and let her know the extent of his desire. She moved her body against him. Pressing harder and higher, he sandwiched her face between his hands and kissed her fiercely.

An instant later, he was gone, swallowed by the darkness.

The only sounds Elizabeth heard were those of her own pounding heart and raspy breathing. And the dripping water hydrant. Those splashing drops landing in the muddy puddle beneath the hydrant were her only remaining link with reality, the only clue that let her know that what had happened was real and not one of her fantasies.

She stumbled back into her house, up the stairs, and into her bedroom. She closed the door, leaning against it weakly and gulping for breath. She lifted a hand to her lips. They were still warm and damp. They stung slightly. She could feel that they were swollen and beard-abraded.

It had been real. It had happened. But how? Why? Why had she permitted it?

Because she was human. She was a woman who had known passion. Her needs hadn't died with John Burke. Her natural, physical desires hadn't been sealed in the coffin with him. In and of themselves they weren't shameful. But the manner in which she chose to satisfy them could be. Trysts with a neighbor in the backyard in the middle of the night weren't a proper means by which to cool her blood. If it was going to run this hot, this unpredictably, she'd have to find an outlet.

As though driven by the muses—or the devil—she crossed to her small wicker desk and took out a notebook and pen. The ink flowed from the ballpoint like blood from an open vein. The room grew cold, but she didn't stop long enough even to put on her robe. She didn't cease her frantic writing until her stable fantasy and the one about the faceless stranger had been converted from images in her mind to words on paper.

Afterward she slept soundly and dreamlessly. In the morning, she called Lilah before she could change her mind.

Only after she had had several hours to think about it did she begin to have doubts. Lilah, to be sure, had been delighted with Elizabeth's decision to submit her fantasies for publication. She had driven over immediately to pick up the pages Elizabeth had written the night before.

She snatched them from her sister's hand. "I'm not going to give you time to change your mind. What made you decide to do it?"

Elizabeth was glad that the Monday-morning rush back into routine prevented an in-depth discussion of her motivations. Not that she would share with anyone what had happened in the backyard last night. She would go to her grave with that secret intact.

"I can use the extra money," she told Lilah by way of explanation. "If you think they're publishable, send them off. But you won't hurt my feelings by telling me they're not."

"I can't wait to read them," Lilah said, licking her lips as though anticipating a feast.

All morning, Elizabeth expected to get a phone call from her sister. When lunchtime arrived and she still hadn't heard from her, she reasoned that her writing had been terrible and that Lilah was trying to think of a tactful way to tell her.

There was little going on in the hotel, so her business was slow. After she'd eaten her fruit and cheese lunch, she began thumbing through order catalogues. When the small bell over her door tinkled, finally announcing a customer, she glanced up with a ready smile.

It congealed on her lips when she saw Thad Randolph standing inside her shop. She almost fell off her high stool, which she sat on behind the counter between customers. For endless moments they stared at each other.

At last, he said, "Hi."

Her feet touched the floor, but she still didn't trust herself to stand. Her knees were actually trembling. She smoothed down her skirt with damp palms. Her cheeks were hot. Her earlobes began to throb. "Hello."

After another tense silence, he dragged his eyes away from her and took in his surroundings. "I've window-shopped through the glass, but I've never been inside your store. It's nice."

"Thank you."

"It smells good."

"I sell potpourri and sachets." She indicated a basket filled with little lace pillows stuffed with dried flowers and spices.

Had she really been in this man's arms last night? Naked except for a sheer batiste nightgown? Moving against him yearningly, kissing him in a way that, even now, made her giddy? And were they now calmly discussing sachets? Saturday night she'd felt rebuffed because he hadn't made a pass at her. He'd been almost too nice. Well, he hadn't been nice last night. But instead of being angry, she was now confused.

She watched him move toward a display of scented stationery. He picked up one of the gift-wrapped boxes and sniffed it. "Chanel?" he asked her over his shoulder.

She nodded dumbly. On whom had he smelled Chanel, she wondered.

He replaced the stationery and wandered toward the shelves stocked with an array of chocolates. Her clever display was eye-catching, but it didn't quite warrant the undivided attention he gave it.

"The open box is there for you to sample," she said to fill the teeming silence.

"Good merchandising, but no thanks."

From there he moved to the crystal pin boxes and perfume bottles, then to the lacquered jewelry boxes, then to the satin lingerie travel cases, then to the lace-bound volumes of poetry.

Elizabeth became entranced by the manner in which he picked up and handled the merchandise. He had large, capable, manly hands that were sprinkled with dark hair. Yet they weren't bashful about touching even the most delicate filigree trinket.

"What's the key for?"

Startled by the sudden question, Elizabeth yanked her gaze from his hands to his face. "Uh, it goes with the diary."

"Oh, I see."

He picked up the book with the padded satin cover and pushed the tiny gold key into the lock. Something about the surety with which he inserted the key into the slot made Elizabeth light-headed. She caught herself swaying on the stool. He laid the diary back on the shelf. She took a deep breath. He turned to face her, but remained disconcertingly silent.

"Is there . . . Did you need . . . Are you looking for anything in particular?"

He cleared his throat and glanced away. "Yes. I need something nice."

"Oh?" She wanted to add "For whom?" but thought better of it.

"A very special gift."

"Any special occasion?"

He coughed. "Well, actually, yes. I need to reestablish a bygone relationship." He moved to stand directly in front of the glass showcase she was sitting behind. "The sooner, the better. If I don't, I'm afraid that I won't be able to stop with a kiss next time."

Elizabeth kept her eyes trained on the square, blunt edge of his chin. But he didn't move away and he didn't say anything more. It became obvious that he expected her to make the next move, so she painstakingly raised her eyes to meet his. "You didn't stop with a kiss this time."

"No," he said softly, "I didn't, did I? Do you need an apology, Elizabeth?"

She shook her head. "I'd rather not talk about it at all."

"You don't want an explanation?"

"I'm not sure there is an explanation for something like that. It just"—she made a helpless gesture —"happened."

"I didn't plan it."

"I know."

"I don't want you to think that I crossed our backyards with a wallbanger in mind."

She sucked in a quick little breath. "I don't."

They said nothing for a moment, then he asked, "Why were you so hostile yesterday at the market?"

"I was annoyed."

"Why?"

"I don't know exactly," she said, meaning it. "I guess because I want to get my own dates. I don't want my children to recruit them for me. I wanted to make it clear to you that I didn't expect you to ask me out again. Maybe I went overboard to get my point across."

"You did."

"I realize that now. I'm sorry I overreacted."

"No need to apologize. I overreacted too. You made me mad as hell. I shouldn't have said what I did, though. That was uncalled for."

"Please," she said, shaking her head. "I understand."

He released a long breath. "Anyway, when I drove in last night and saw that your sprinkler was on, I thought I'd do you a favor and turn it off. I didn't expect to see you standing there. Especially wearing nothing but a thin nightgown." His eyes turned a shade darker. "That came as quite a shock to my system."

"You don't think I went out like that to attract your attention, do you?"

"No."

"Because I didn't. I heard the water running and realized I'd forgotten to turn it off. If it hadn't been so late I would never have gone outside in my nightgown. And if it hadn't been necessary, I wouldn't have gone outside at all."

"I understand."

If he understood, she'd do well to shut up while she was ahead. This was one of those bad situations that could only get worse by saying too much. "What did you have in mind?" she asked.

"Just to kiss you. Nothing more than that, I swear. But then you started kissing me back. I felt your breasts against my chest and, damn, they felt good. I had to— What's the matter?"

"I meant to buy," she said croakingly. "What did you have in mind to buy for the gift to give your . . . your lady?"

"Oh, that. Well, let's see." He slid his hands into his trousers pockets, a gesture which flipped back his jacket. The front of his shirt was smoothly filled out by the muscled chest beneath it. The front of his trousers was filled out by the bulging . . .

Elizabeth guiltily jerked her eyes back up to his chest and detected the dark cloud of hair through the fine cloth. It was the first time she'd ever seen him in a necktie except from a distance. Did he always dress up for his afternoon affairs?

"What do you suggest?" he asked her.

Flustered, she couldn't think of a single item in her inventory. She gazed around the shop as though seeing it for the first time. She couldn't remember what anything was called or how much it cost. Finally, raking together enough words to form a coherent thought, she made several suggestions, none of which appealed to him.

"No, she's not the bookish type," he said, when Elizabeth suggested a slender volume of Shakespeare's sonnets.

No, she wouldn't be. Of course not. Mistresses rarely were. A man didn't go to his mistress, especially one he hadn't seen in quite a while, for cerebral stimulation.

"What about some of this frilly underwear?" Thad was rifling through the circular rack of lingerie. "Do women really enjoy wearing this kind of thing? Or do men just wish they did?"

Her anger at him surged to the forefront again. Why was he bringing his sordid business to her? If he wanted to buy a sexy negligee for his illicit lover, why did it have to be from her?

"Some women do," she snapped. The emphasis she placed on the first word indicated that the women who did enjoy wearing such garments were of questionable virtue.

"Do you?"

Her eyes swung up to his. They were daring her to lie. She rose to meet the challenge. Besides, her son had already informed him that she did. "Sometimes. If I'm in the mood."

"How often does the mood strike you?"

Her middle grew warm. The warmth spread upward. It filled her breasts and collected in their tightening nipples. Had he noticed them poking against the front of her blouse? Was he remembering the way his tongue had lashed them, making them wet through the cloth of her nightgown?

"That varies from woman to woman," she said.

He turned and began looking through the garments, sliding the hangers along the metal rack. The sound they made was as irritating to Elizabeth as fingernails on a chalkboard.

"This is pretty." He pulled an article out and held it up. "What's it called?"

"A teddy."

His lips formed a wide, wolfish smile. "No wonder. A man could really cuddle up with it."

She failed to see the humor and barely curbed the impulse to snatch the teddy away from him. "Do you want it or not? It's sixty dollars." He whistled softly. "Isn't she worth it?" Elizabeth asked snidely.

"Oh, yes, she's definitely worth it."

The pitch and depth of his voice made her toes curl. "Shall I wrap it up?"

"Not so fast. I haven't decided yet. Sell me on it."

He dropped the teddy on the countertop. Elizabeth's temper rose a degree. Either he wanted the damn thing or he didn't. But knowing she couldn't afford to sacrifice a sixty-dollar sale, particularly on a slow day, she picked up the teddy and began to enumerate its various merits.

"It's made of one-hundred-percent silk."

He took a pinch of the fabric between his fingers and rubbed it, exactly as he had done the strand of her hair the night before. "Very nice. It's sheer, almost transparent. Is that a problem?"

"Pardon?"

"Does anything show through?"

"Isn't it supposed to?"

"In the bedroom, yes. But not if she's wearing it under her clothes."

"Oh. Well, no, that shouldn't be a problem."

"Okay," he said, "what about the color? What do you call that?"

"Nude."

"That figures. What about size?"

"What size is she?" Forty-four double D, she thought peevishly.

"About your size. Hold it up to you."

She hesitated, but not wanting to appear prudish, she slipped the teddy off the hanger. Laying the straps on her shoulders, she held it in place against her. "It's stretchy. It should fit if she's a thirty-two or thirty-four."

"Thirty-two or thirty-four what?"

"Bra size."

"Ahh." Thad squinted his eyes and let them linger

on the bra cups of the teddy that were conforming to her shape. "That should be okay. Do these come undone?"

He raised his hand to the row of pearl buttons down the front. With a flick of his fingers, the first two popped open. Their eyes sprang together just as quickly.

Elizabeth dropped the garment onto the countertop. "Have you decided?"

"What does this do?"

Entranced, she watched as his finger slowly and deliberately followed the high cut leg of the teddy to the tapering point that brought front and back together. A moan pressed against the inside of her lips. "It unsnaps," she answered in an unnaturally husky voice.

"What for?"

Distressed beyond the breaking point, she cried, "What do you think?"

"Hmm, that's handy. And these are for stockings?" He ran his index finger down one lacy suspender.

"Yes. But they're removable."

"Throw in a pair of lacy stockings and I'll take it."

"Cash or credit card?"

"Credit card."

"Fine."

He had her so badly rattled that she could barely write up the ticket. She moved the shuttle so hard that her machine nearly ate his credit card. T. D. Randolph. She wondered if his name was Thaddeus and what the *D* stood for, then cursed herself for wondering. She didn't give a damn what his full name was.

"Gift wrap?" she asked ungraciously as she rolled up the sinful teddy and stockings in pink tissue paper.

"That won't be necessary."

I'll bet. He was probably going straight to his lover's arms. Unwrapping the gift would only take precious time and delay things.

"Thank you," he said, accepting the Fantasy shopping bag from her outstretched hand.

"You're welcome."

"See you at home."

Not if I can help it. She nodded coolly and averted her head before he was even out the door. But she surreptitiously looked through the paned glass and watched him leave the hotel with a carefree gait which she found disgustingly cocky.

At least he wasn't conducting his shabby, reconciliatory affair in a room of the Hotel Cavanaugh. One of those motels out on the interstate would be more his style.

She turned her back on the lobby and slapped his credit card receipt into her cash drawer. When the tiny gold bell over her door jingled again, she thought he had come back for something. Wearing a frown as discouraging as a "Do Not Disturb" sign, she turned to confront him.

"Oh, hello!" she exclaimed with chagrin.

Six

Adam Cavanaugh asked, "Am I intruding?"

"No, of course not, Mr. Cavanaugh. I was just, uh
. . ." This man, on whom she wanted to make a
good impression, caught her for the second time in
the midst of her foolish daydreams. "I was looking
through some catalogues."

"You seemed lost in thought."

"Yes, I was. Please come in and sit down." This
time he had come alone.

"I can only stay a minute." Unabashedly he helped
himself to the box of sample chocolates, licking his
fingers with complete unselfconsciousness. "I'm between appointments. I would have dropped by sooner,
but my calendar has been full."

"I'm sure you've been awfully busy."

"I was wondering if we could have dinner together
Saturday night."

"Dinner?" she repeated stupidly. Dinner with Adam
Cavanaugh, international playboy and one of the
world's most eligible bachelors? *Her?*

"Are you free that night? If not, we can make it—"

"No, I'm free," she said hastily. "Dinner on Saturday will be fine."

"Great. I find business discussions much more enjoyable if they're conducted with a beautiful woman over dinner." He flashed her a Hollywood-worthy smile. "I'll get your address from the file and pick you up at seven-thirty."

"Or I could meet you somewhere," she suggested, not wanting him to go out of his way.

"I'd rather pick you up. Seven-thirty on Saturday?"

"Yes, fine."

"See you then, Elizabeth."

For a full five minutes after he left, she couldn't believe he'd actually been there and made a dinner date. She pinched herself several times to make sure she wasn't in her dream world. He was so handsome, so charming, so well dressed and immaculately groomed, so everything that any woman could possibly want. And he had invited the Widow Burke to dinner!

What would she wear?

Her sluggish Monday was compensated for by a hectic Tuesday when a regional association of veterinarians held a two-day seminar in the hotel. Their business kept her well occupied Wednesday morning as well. By the time the animal doctors checked out at noon, Fantasy needed a facelift.

She straightened the shelves and reorganized the merchandise which had been displaced by browsers. The mindless chore required little concentration. It was raining outside. Even indoors, the atmosphere was gloomy. She lit scented candles in the shop to make it appear warmer and more cheerful to potential customers.

It was a perfect day for snuggling in front of a

fireplace with a good book. Or for napping. Elizabeth grew sleepy. Her mind began to drift . . .

The curving stone staircase was dim. The stairs were uneven. The footsteps of ancestors had eroded them. I picked my way carefully, hoping not to spill anything I was carrying on the tray.

At the landing, meager gray light was coming through one narrow window. Silver streams of rain trickled down the cloudy glass. Propping the heavy tray on my hip, I tapped on the oaken door at the end of the hall. He called for me to come in. As I pushed open the heavy door, my heart began to pound. It had done so each time I entered the spare bedroom where our "guest" was confined to bed.

He'd been residing under our roof for almost two weeks. I vividly recalled the afternoon I had heard his biplane circling overhead and had run from the kitchen into the yard. The airplane had been trailing a plume of black smoke. He had managed to land it and climb out safely before it crashed and burst into flames.

My father, who had been working in the fields, also saw the crash. Together we ran toward the fiery wreckage. The pilot had crawled free, but was obviously injured. Between us, we carried him inside and up the stairs to this room.

He was American. Through teeth clenched in pain, he instructed Father to douse the fire so that the smoke wouldn't signal the Germans. He spoke only a smattering of French; we spoke no English. But he made himself understood before losing consciousness. Father hurried to do as he'd been told and left me to take care of the injured pilot.

I removed his goggles and leather flight cap. As I

sponged the grime off his face, my heart began to flutter. He was extremely handsome, with thick curly brown hair that fell over his brow. My fingers became clumsy when I tried to remove his clothing, but I had no choice but to do so. A dark red stain was spreading out on the sheet beneath him.

I was to learn later that he'd been hit by a German machine gun during a dog fight. The rest of his squadron had been shot down. The bullet had ripped a hole in his side just above his waist. I cleaned the wound and bound it. His unconscious moans brought tears to my eyes.

He would recover, but it would be a long time before he could return to active duty or even be moved to a military hospital. Since Father worked from dawn till dark, the responsibility of tending the American pilot had fallen to me.

As I entered the room now, he was lying against the headboard, propped up by pillows. I lowered my gaze from his bare chest because each time I looked at it, a shameful, damp heat collected in my womanhood. The sight of him made my breasts tingle. His clothes had been so bloodstained that I'd had to destroy them. All but the long white silk scarf which I had carefully unwound from his neck and which now lay beneath the pillow of my own bed.

I knew that he lay naked beneath the sheet. I also knew what he looked like naked, for I had sponged his body repeatedly when he was wracked with fever and delirium.

Made timid by his scrutiny, I asked him if he felt like eating and he answered yes. The floorboards of the ancient house creaked as I walked across them to the narrow bed. Lowering the tray to the nightstand, I sat down on the edge of the bed, mindful not to let my hip bump against his thigh, which was clearly outlined beneath the thin sheet.

My hand trembled as I spooned the soup into his mouth. Smiling, he complimented me on how good it tasted. I blotted his lips with the napkin after each bite. He ate all the soup.

Before leaving him, I lit the candle on the night-stand to alleviate the gloom caused by the rain which could be heard dripping heavily from the eaves. Standing beside his bed, my hands nervously clasped together in front of me, I asked if there was anything else I could do for him.

He said nothing, but raised his hand and placed it in the curve of my waist. I felt his touch through my clothing, as hot as a poker. Applying but slight pressure, he urged me back down beside him. His sparkling eyes entranced me. I was helpless to resist them. He lifted his hand and stroked my cheek with the backs of his fingers. He playfully tugged at the tendrils of hair that had escaped my bun. He told me the Americans called it the Gibson-girl style and he laughed at my accented efforts to repeat the words.

Then his hand moved to my throat and the high collar of my shirtwaist. He ran his finger over the lace, around the cameo brooch which had belonged to my late mother, and down the row of buttons. One by one, he unfastened them.

My heartbeat drummed against his palm when he reached into my shirtwaist and covered my breast with his hand, taking all the fullness within the gentle grasp of his strong fingers. Heat and confusion overwhelmed me. I swayed dizzily when he touched the tip of my breast and blushed with shame and pleasure when it jutted hard against the stroking pad of his thumb.

He curled his free hand around my neck and pulled my head down onto the pillows next to his. He kissed me. I was shocked when his lips parted and he pressed his tongue into my mouth. I had never realized that mouths could be so intimate. Mating was a natural occurrence on the farm, but I had assumed that human beings approached reproduction with the same attitude of detachment as the animals. Never had I guessed that one's heart could beat so fast, or that one's blood could flow so hotly, so thickly. I hadn't known that such pleasure could be derived from coupling.

His hands got inside my clothing and touched soft, secret parts of my body that I barely skimmed with my washing cloth. I had learned in church that touching "there" was sinful. But I didn't think about sin or my father or the chores waiting to be done. I thought of nothing but the American and the beautiful sensations his stroking hands were giving me.

I heard myself moan when he palmed the soft nest of hair between my thighs. His fingers, deft and sure, discovered a deep pool of liquid desire inside me.

In a rough, grating voice, he asked me to touch him, making himself understood by guiding my hand. It seemed an odd request since I'd been touching him for days. But as my hand slid beneath the sheet and moved over his smooth skin and the patches of crisp body hair, I knew that this kind of touching was different. He was different. Warm, but with another type of fever. His breathing was rapid, but not with delirium.

He bunched my skirts around my waist and pulled me over him. I wanted to remind him of his wound, but he pushed aside my camisole and put *his mouth to my breast. He pressed his tongue against my nipple. I couldn't speak. I could do nothing but open myself to the thru—*

When the telephone rang, Elizabeth jumped in startled reaction. By an act of will she reduced the furious pace of her heart. She took several deep breaths. Her hand was shaking when she reached for the receiver. "Hello."

"Hi, it's me. What's wrong?"

It was Lilah. "Nothing."

"You sound funny."

"I'm busy."

"Busy writing more fantasies, I hope. Lizzie, they're terrific!"

When three days had passed and Lilah still hadn't called, Elizabeth had assumed that her writing had seemed too amateurish to be published or that Lilah simply hadn't liked her fantasies. Either way, she had been both relieved and chagrined that her writing career had been so short-lived.

"You don't have to say that just to spare my feelings," she told her sister now.

"I'm not. My Lord, Lizzie, I had no idea you were so imaginatively erotic. I read the two fantasies a dozen times apiece and was thoroughly entertained each time."

"But you're my sister and you love me. It's natural that you—"

"Right. I *wanted* them to be good, so I questioned my own judgment, even though I knew I was right. To make sure, I had four other people here at the hospital read them."

"You didn't!"

"Relax. I didn't say who wrote them. They'd never believe it was mousy little you anyway."

"Thanks," Elizabeth said dryly.

"Anyway, suffice it to say that both the women and the men who read them—"

"You gave them to *men*?"

"Women don't have the fantasy market cornered, you know," Lilah argued. "I thought it would be valuable to see if the fantasies worked for men, too, and they certainly did. They're on their way to New York already. The manuscripts, not the men," she added, laughing.

"You've already mailed them?"

"Yes, so you wouldn't have a chance to talk me out of it. I typed them myself. Made hundreds of errors, my hands were so slick with sweat. When do I get to read more?"

"More? Who said there would be more?"

"I did. Talent like yours isn't exhausted with just two fantasies."

"I'm not sure it takes talent, and I don't know when or if I'll have time to write any more." Shyly she said, "I have a date Saturday night."

"You're kidding!" Lilah squealed. "With who? The hunk with the chicken coop?"

"It wasn't a chicken coop. The pen was for a litter of Irish setters. His name is Thad Randolph, and, no, my date isn't with him." She hadn't told Lilah about last Saturday night and the Fall Festival because her sister would have jumped to the wrong conclusion. Lilah would have hypothesized that Thad had gone on her account and not to please the children. "Adam Cavanaugh invited me to have dinner with him."

"Really? Well, my dear sister, that should be fodder for another story. Remember every single, scintillating detail."

"Lilah, it's only *dinner*."

"Which, if you play your cards right, can last through breakfast." At Elizabeth's gasp of outrage, Lilah said, "Don't get all huffy. It's about time you started living some of your fantasies. Have fun, just don't fall in love with Cavanaugh."

Lilah hung up soon after winning Elizabeth's promise to think about writing more fantasies. Elizabeth was surprised to see that she'd kept the shop open five minutes past closing time and locked up quickly. Mrs. Alder got upset if she was too late.

Because of the rain, traffic was a nightmare. Then, before she could even get out of the car at home, Megan and Matt closed in on her with a problem.

"Mom, something terrible has happened to Thad," Megan said theatrically.

Edging her children aside, Elizabeth got out of the car and shut the door. "What do you mean, something terrible has happened to Thad? Good-bye, Mrs. Alder," she called to the departing baby-sitter. "Now, what's this about Thad?" Elizabeth asked her children who would have made a professional mourning duo look cheerful.

"We think he's dead or something."

Matt was so somber, Elizabeth covered a laugh with a cough. "What gave you that idea?"

"Because his car is there, but he doesn't answer his door when we knock."

"He could be out on his motorcycle."

"It's in the garage."

"Well, maybe he just doesn't want company." Or, more likely, he *has* company, Elizabeth thought. She hadn't seen him since he'd strolled out of Fantasy on Monday with the gift for his mistress swinging in the shopping bag in his large hand.

Megan was shaking her head. "We can see breakfast dishes on the kitchen table. He doesn't like messes. He told me that a long time ago."

"He probably just didn't feel like cleaning up today."

"Or maybe he's dead. Maybe somebody came in and stabbed him or something. Then it'll be our fault for not checking."

Where did Matt come up with these macabre ideas? Easy, she thought. He took after her.

"Come on, Mom. You've got to go see."

Each child had taken her by the hand and was pulling her across the yard. "I'm sure there's a logical explanation." She dug in her heels, but the children were genuinely worried. If she didn't relieve their concern, she'd never hear the end of it. They'd bug her about it until she relented. "Oh, all right."

The wisdom of her decision was again put to the test when she raised her hand to knock on his back door. She hesitated, but one glance down at Megan and Matt prompted her to knock firmly. She waited several seconds and, hearing no sound of approaching footsteps, knocked again.

"See, Mom, he doesn't answer."

"He's dead."

"He's not dead," she emphasized to her morbid son. "In fact, I'm sure there's nothing wrong." Cupping her hands around her eyes, she peered through the screen. As the children had said, the kitchen table, which she could see through the connecting doorway, was cluttered with what appeared to be the dishes of several meals.

"Go in and see. The door is unlocked."

"Megan, I can't just walk into a man's house!"

"How come?"

The inquiry in their eyes was so innocent and earnest that Elizabeth found herself groping for an answer. "It isn't polite, that's why." What she couldn't explain to her children was that Mr. Randolph wouldn't want to be disturbed if he was frolicking in bed with a girlfriend or sleeping off a drinking binge or . . . Few other possibilities came immediately to mind. In spite of herself, she was mystified. What *was* he doing in there?

"What if Thad's sick and you don't help him?"

"Yeah, he might die and it'd be your fault. Your fault, Mom."

"All right!" she cried. Laying on a guilt trip worked every time and how well her kids knew it. She opened the screen door and then the wooden one, finding both, as Megan had told her, unlocked. She took one step inside. Both children followed close on her heels. "No, you two stay here." She didn't want her children to see their idol in a compromising position— or any kind of position—with a member of the opposite sex.

"We want to come too."

"No. Stay here. I'll find out if anything is wrong and then come right back."

As a safety precaution against disobedience, she latched the screen door behind her, then tiptoed across the enclosed porch. Before entering the kitchen, she called his name. Her voice sounded unnaturally loud. It echoed through the empty house. He was probably out with a friend and this was a gross violation of his privacy which she'd have to explain to him later.

But his being out with a friend didn't explain the dirty dishes that were scattered on the table and piled high in the sink. He wouldn't let his kitchen get this messy unless he had a very good reason.

Not knowing exactly how the rooms of the house were laid out, she followed her nose toward the front door and called his name again. The living room, she discovered, was tastefully decorated. Nothing fancy certainly, but contemporary and arranged with a sense of style. Several magazines were neatly stacked on the coffee table. *Newsweek, Time, Esquire.* Not a naked girl among them.

"He probably keeps those in the bedroom," she whispered to herself.

Encroaching dusk had made the dark day even darker. The rain she'd driven home in had caught up with her and was now beginning to patter against the windows. She hadn't turned on any lights. The large rooms were gloomy. This whole thing was getting spooky.

"Mr. Randolph? Thad?" She paused to listen. Receiving no answer, she gladly turned and headed back toward the kitchen.

But she'd taken no more than a few steps when she heard the low moan. She froze, pausing to be sure she'd heard right. Yes, there it was again. Louder this time.

Her heart began bumping crazily. Was it a moan of pain or passion? Agony or ecstasy? Possibly both? Good Lord, she didn't want to know. But her children would never let it rest until she found out.

Reversing her direction, she started down the hallway. As she drew nearer an open door, she could hear the whisper of cloth against cloth. Bed linens to be sure, but two bodies or one? She took a deep breath and peeped around the door, jerking her head back quickly after registering what she had seen.

The room was unmistakably Thad's bedroom. Against the wall opposite the door was a king-size bed. He was lying on it. Thankfully alone. Though not restfully.

In the split second she had allowed herself to look into the room, it became apparent that he was ill.

His arms and legs were moving restlessly and his head was thrashing from side to side on his pillow.

Elizabeth garnered her courage and entered the bachelor's bedroom with the trepidation of a young soldier going into battle for the first time. One did one's duty.

"Thad?"

She wasn't surprised that he didn't hear her. Her voice was quaking and hushed. His moaning, which had grown louder, easily drowned it out. He slung one arm out to his side and gave the sheet a vicious kick.

He was naked.

She was spared from seeing everything by one corner of the baby-blue sheet, which fortuitously was twisted around his hips. One bare foot and calf were poking over the edge of the bed. The other leg was covered, but clearly defined beneath the sheet, which was pulled taut. His chest was bare. His concave stomach was heaving up and down with labored breathing. His navel—

Elizabeth glanced away from his navel, but not before noting that it was sexy and deep and surrounded by a whorl of dark hair. A silky thread of hair perfectly bisected his torso and connected his wide chest to his narrow abdomen. His nipples should have been relaxed. They weren't.

She tiptoed toward the bed as though a slumbering beast lay there and not a harmless man. His eyelids were closed but they were fluttering spasmodically. He mumbled something that she couldn't understand and let out another deep groan.

Moved to pity, she raised a knee onto the bed and leaned over him. "Thad? Are you ill?"

One of his hands reached out blindly. The other one—

She hadn't noticed *that* until he covered it with his hand, though how it had escaped her attention she couldn't imagine. Maybe she *had* noticed it, but her mind had refused to acknowledge it. It had no choice now.

Her eyes were too dry to blink. She began panting through her parted lips. A ringing sound, as loud as Quasimodo's bells, filled her head. She felt faint.

He flailed his arm again. His fist landed solidly against her chest. His fingers uncurled and touched the softness of her breast. That must have stunned him out of his troubled dream, because his eyes popped open. He stared up at her, as astonished to see her standing beside his bed as she was to have his large hand covering her breast.

He snatched his hand away from the lower part of his body and, with the other, yanked the sheet up to his waist. Both ignored, or tried to, that the sheet was tented over his lap.

"What are you doing here?" He was hoarse. He ran his tongue over parched lips in an attempt to moisten them.

It took several attempts before she could speak. When she did, she could only stutter. "I—I— The children— Are you sick?"

He laid his forearm over his eyes. "I'll be all right."

His macho refusal to admit that he was ill infuriated her. "Are you sick or not?"

"Yes, I'm sick," he muttered. "Flu, I guess. You'd better get out before you catch it and give it to the kids."

"Do you have fever?"

"I don't know. Do I?"

He lowered his arm. Elizabeth hesitated for just a moment before laying a cool hand on his forehead.

It was clammy, but still warm. "I think you have some."

"It broke earlier. I started sweating. Kicked the covers off." Beyond the foot of the bed, a soggy bedspread and blanket were lying in a heap on the floor.

"Do you have a thermometer?"

"In the bathroom cabinet."

Grateful for any excuse to put distance between them, she left his bedside and went into the adjoining bathroom. On the second shelf of the cabinet over the basin she located a thermometer. Resisting the urge to investigate what else might be found in the cabinet, she carried it and a plastic bottle of aspirin into the bedroom.

He had straightened the sheet and pulled it up to an inch or so above his waist. Both legs were now covered, but his chest was still bare and his nipples were still erect. In as detached a manner as possible under the circumstances, she shook down the mercury in the thermometer. Leaning forward, she waited for him to open his mouth, then laid the thermometer under his tongue.

"Have you taken any of these?" She held out the bottle of aspirin. He shook his head no. Giving him an exasperated look, she said, "I'll be right back. Keep that thermometer under your tongue."

Megan and Matt were dancing with impatience when she opened the screen door. "You were right," she began before they had time to fire their thousand and one questions at her, "Thad is sick."

"Can we come in and visit him?"

"No."

"You're s'pposed to visit sick friends. That's what they say in Sunday school."

"But not when your friend is contagious. You could catch the flu."

"You could catch it too. How come you can visit Thad and we can't?"

"Because I'm a mother and mothers don't catch diseases the way kids do." She hoped they would buy that. They didn't.

In unison they said, "But, Mom—"

"No arguments." Her stern expression silenced them. "I'm going to clean up his kitchen and heat some soup for him. While I'm doing that, why don't you check on Penny and the puppies? Make sure they have fresh water."

Having dispatched them, she filled a clean glass with cold water and returned to the bedroom. She caught Thad in the process of taking the thermometer out of his mouth. He passed it to her. "What does it say? I never could read the damn thing."

"One hundred point four," she told him as she shook the mercury down again before returning the thermometer to its plastic case. "Take two aspirin." He dutifully swallowed the tablets with the water she'd brought for him. "Will you remember to take two more around ten o'clock?"

"I'll try."

As soon as he'd swallowed the aspirins, his head weakly dropped back onto the pillow. Elizabeth noticed that it was hard and lumpy and that the pillowcase was damp with sweat. "Would you like for me to change your bed?"

He glanced down his body, then back up at her. "No."

She didn't argue. Actually, she was relieved. Not that she would have minded the chore. But just the thought of getting a naked Thad in and out of the bed left her feeling weak-kneed. "How about switching pillows then?"

He let her do that, raising his head long enough for

her to replace the pillow with the one she found on the far side of the bed. "Where are your extra blankets?"

"Linen closet in the hall, but I'm hot."

"If you don't stay covered, you'll get chilled." Maybe that's why his nipples were still hard.

She located the linen closet and found his sheets and towels neatly folded on the shelves. Bringing a blanket back with her, she whipped it high over the bed and let it float down to cover him. She did not pat it into place. "Rest while I heat the soup. I assume you have a can of soup in the house."

He nodded but waved his hand in protest. "You've done enough, Elizabeth. I just need to sleep this off. Tomorrow I'll be back at work."

"If you are, then the day after that you'll be in the hospital." She aimed a finger at him. "Stay put. I'll be back shortly."

While the chicken noodle soup was simmering on the range, she rinsed the dirty dishes and loaded them in the dishwasher. She also sponged off the countertops and table and replaced food items that had been left out. The soup was ready by the time she had finished. She ladled some into a bowl and placed it on a tray along with a glass of orange juice, a spoon, and a paper napkin.

It was when she paused on the threshold of his bedroom, holding the laden tray, that her most recent fantasy elbowed its way into her consciousness. This wasn't the French countryside. She wasn't a farmer's virgin daughter, and Thad wasn't a wounded fighter pilot, but the uncanny similarity between the fantasy and this reality made her shiver.

She moved to his bedside, set the tray on the nightstand, and switched on the lamp. The bulb was hardly brighter than candlelight. The soft light fell on Thad's face. He was dozing. His eyelashes cast sweeping shadows on his cheekbones. His chest rose and fell faintly with each breath. The aspirin was working.

She spoke his name softly. His eyes came open. They penetrated hers in a way that was almost sexual. A trill of sensation spiraled up out of her belly like a rising phoenix. "Do you feel like eating something?"

"I guess so." She offered him the glass of cold orange juice. He drank it down in one swallow.

"You should have been drinking more liquids," she chided gently as she passed him the napkin. He seemed at a loss as to what to do with it, so he just held it in his hand.

"I didn't feel like getting up for anything."

"Matt and Megan are seeing to Penny and the puppies."

"Thanks. I knew the puppies wouldn't starve, but I was worried about Penny. I came down with this yesterday morning."

So he'd probably kept his date Monday afternoon, Elizabeth reasoned. She started to ask him how his lady friend had liked the teddy, but she really didn't want to know. "Can you feed yourself?"

"If you'll hold the tray, I think I can manage."

She gingerly lowered herself to the edge of the bed and lifted the tray onto her lap. He bent over it, supporting himself on one elbow. Lifting the spoon awkwardly, he dipped it into the soup and slurped it into his mouth.

"It's good. Thank you, Elizabeth."

"You're welcome."

He ate most of the soup before setting down the spoon. "That's all I want for now."

"All right." She moved the tray off her lap and returned it to the nightstand.

Before she could lower her arms, she felt his hand at her waist. It molded itself to her shape and drew her around. "You feel so cool," he murmured.

Elizabeth stared down at him in mute dismay as he rested his head on her thigh and buried his face in the fabric of her skirt. He ground the tousled crown of his head against her stomach.

She went very still and let every feminine, maternal, giving, loving fiber of her being have its way. Easily, her caution was conquered. Then, acting instinctively, she laid her hand against his flushed cheek. He sighed and reached up to cover it with his own. Her other hand smoothed the damp strands of graying hair off his forehead.

After several moments, he raised his head and looked up at her. "Was I dreaming, or did I really kiss you?"

"When?"

"A few minutes ago. When you first came in." He stroked her cheek and toyed with the wisps of hair that had escaped her bun.

"You must have been dreaming."

"I wasn't touching your breast?"

Breathless, she shook her head no. "You sort of socked it."

"No, I remember that. In my dream, I was caressing it, stroking it with my thumb." His eyes traced a hot path from the cameo brooch at her throat to the row of buttons on her blouse. "And you were caressing me."

Remembering the placement of his hand, she went hot all over. "I'd better go. My kids will be wondering . . ."

He lay back against the pillow. She picked up the

tray and all but ran from the room. Her hands were shaking, the very hands she had wanted to use to draw his head to her breasts and let it rest there for as long as he wished.

She quickly cleared off the tray and reloaded it with a pitcher of ice water and a clean glass. She avoided looking at Thad directly as she set the tray on the nightstand.

"Don't forget to take the aspirin. And drink plenty of water. I won't bother you again unless you call for help. And please do if you need to. Well," she said, clasping her hands together and nervously backing toward the door, "bye."

She turned to flee, but he caught her hand. "Elizabeth, I'm glad you came by. Thanks for everything." He ran his thumb over the inside of her wrist. "But in a way, I wish you hadn't woken me up when you did. I'd like to know how that dream ended."

Seven

I trembled before him, more terrified for my virtue than for my life. At least dying had dignity. Being the sexual slave of a pirate king didn't.

Coarse, bearded, foul-smelling men had kidnapped me from my bedroom and carried me, bound hand and foot, to this ship. I was still blindfolded, but I knew we were on the open seas now. The creaking deck heaved beneath my feet and I could hear the popping canvas sails above me.

The wind was high. My cloak billowed around me and plastered my thin white nightgown to my naked body. I shivered, not with cold, but with the intuitive knowledge that he, the commander of this band of cutthroats who had ordered my abduction, was standing not far away, complacently observing me like a malicious cat with a trapped mouse.

Not to appear cowed, I lifted my chin a notch higher. He could abuse me, even kill me, but he'd never break my spirit. His dark laughter mingled with the wind. Seconds later I felt the vibration of

his approaching footsteps through the soles of my
bare feet. My heart went wild with anxiety, but I
maintained the proud posture that governesses had
drilled into me from infancy.

My head was snapped forward when he jerked
the blindfold from my eyes. I flung back my hair
and glared into his face. But my hostile stare turned
into a gaping mask of surprise. I knew the pirate
king! Had known him all my life. He was the
wastrel second son of the family who lived on the
neighboring estate, the one reputed to be a gam-
bler and ruthless womanizer. Because of his fla-
grant disregard for propriety, his family had dis-
owned him years ago. His name was rarely spoken
in polite company, and only then in whispers. Now,
here he was, my captor.

He laughed at my astonishment. Then he informed me in a voice laced with menace that he
was avenging an ancient wrong my father had
done him. Sneering, the pirate slid a saber out of
the leather scabbard that was buckled around his
lean hips. Thinking that he meant to kill me on
the spot, I flinched when he made one downward
swipe with the sword.

When I realized that I was still alive and apparently unharmed, I opened my eyes, only to discover that he had slashed through the ties of my
cloak and that it had pooled around my feet. My
nightgown, growing damp from the sea spray, clung
revealingly to my naked body.

His cold, glittering eyes moved over me, pausing
to stare with interest at my breasts and the triang-
ular shadow between my thighs. He made me
shudder with dread. That's what I told myself. I
didn't want to acknowledge that my trembling had
another, altogether different, source.

I remembered this neighbor as a slender youth. He had since filled out, come into his full maturity and developed into a man of impressive form. His wide-sleeved, loose white blouse was opened to the waist, displaying a muscular chest. It was covered with hair, darker even than that on his head. A wide leather belt emphasized the narrowness of his waist. Tall boots, cuffed just above his knees, drew my attention to thighs that were as hard and smooth as the masts of his ship. His manhood, I was revolted to notice, was indecently outlined beneath the tight, thin breeches, which fit better than his skin.

He noted the direction of my gaze and laughed with insufferable conceit. Before I could utter any of the epithets that rushed to my mind, he swept me up against that solid, wide chest. I thrashed my legs as much as my bonds would allow and bowed my back, demanding to know where he was taking me. My struggles only served to delight his men, who cheered their leader on and offered him advice on how to tame me. Their lewd catcalls made my ears and cheeks burn with indignation.

He kicked open the door to his cabin with one booted foot and, after carrying me inside, shut it in the same angry manner. Unceremoniously he dumped me onto the bed. I landed hard, but the bunk was surprisingly soft and wide. In fact the entire room was much more luxurious than I would have expected.

I lay amid the pillows covered in Oriental silk and watched with fearful fascination as he peeled his shirt over his head and nonchalantly tossed it to the floor. Every muscle in his chest and arms rippled beneath his sun-baked skin as he slowly removed his leather belt. Keeping me spellbound with his eyes, he unfastened his breeches.

I gasped with fear and dismay. Smiling, he swaggered toward the bed on which I still lay. Taking a long, double-edged knife from the nearby table, he moved closer and lifted both my bound ankles in one hand. The inescapable knots didn't survive the slash of his knife and my feet came free. He frowned as he inspected the bruises the tight rope had made on my ankles and stroked them with his thumb. Reaching behind me, he freed my hands in the same manner, then drew them forward and inspected my chafed and discolored wrists.

But I was mistaken to think that his feelings toward me might have turned charitable. He was still bent on revenge. In one lightning-quick motion, he pulled me to my feet. I swayed against him, reflexively reaching out for support. He grunted with satisfaction when my breasts flattened against his chest. Tunneling all ten fingers in my hair and settling them against my scalp, he tilted my head back. He smiled triumphantly, then bent his head and covered my lips with his.

I wasn't prepared for the heat that spilled through me like the finest wine. I attributed the tingling in my limbs to having been bound, but I knew that his lips and what they were doing to mine were responsible. His tongue deflowered my mouth as surely as that other part of him, which I felt pressing firmly against my belly, was about to claim my maidenhood.

He grappled with the buttons of my nightgown. Suddenly I came to my senses and began to fight him. Impatient with both my futile efforts and the stubborn buttons, he gathered a handful of the material at the neckline and ripped the gown in two. His other hand manacled my wrists behind my back. After another long, deep kiss that stole my breath and pitched my senses into chaos, he raised his head and raked his eyes down my exposed body.

The change that came over him then was sudden and drastic. In his dark face, I recognized shades of the carefree, happy youth he'd been before his father's unfair comparisons to his older brother had turned him into the roguish ne'er-do-well he had become.

His eyes, no longer cold and implacable, gazed at me with misty longing. In a sad voice, he told me that I was beautiful and sweet and that my innocence was touching. When he raised his hand and covered my breast, he breathed a sigh of such yearning that my heart filled with compassion for him.

He studied the lazy movement of his thumb upon my flesh as he tenderly fanned my nipple into a tight peak. Then, bending his head down low, he stroked the very tip of it with his warm, wet tongue.

His other hand relaxed, releasing my pinioned wrists. I wrapped my arms around his neck and surrendered to the dewy caresses of his mouth. He splayed his hand wide on my derriere and drew me close, close enough to know intimately the extent of his desire. Outside myself now, and acting solely on instinct, I sent my hand down his chest in search of—

"Mrs. Burke?" Elizabeth peered up from beneath the hood of the hair dryer. "Did I startle you? I'm sorry," the manicurist said, smiling apologetically. "I'm ready for you now."

Elizabeth gathered her handbag and followed the manicurist to her table. The visit to the salon had been Lilah's idea. "This is your first official date in ages," she had said. "Treat yourself."

"You're forgetting one crucial point," Elizabeth argued. "Fantasy is open on Saturday afternoons. There won't be time to have my hair done after I close the shop."

Lilah had considered the dilemma for several moments before saying brightly, "I know. I'll mind the store for you."

Elizabeth was far from enthusiastic about the idea. When she was behind the counter in Fantasy, she dressed the part, wearing pastels and lace, soft, romantic clothing reminiscent of a century ago. She doubted Lilah owned anything lacy or pastel. Her black leather pants and vividly striped ponchos would be grossly out of place. However, Lilah had promised to be on her best behavior. Elizabeth would have been ungracious not to accept the unselfish offer. So now she sat docilely while the manicurist worked on her nails, secretly enjoying the respite from her many responsibilities.

Each time she thought of the evening to come, she got butterflies in her stomach. She hadn't seen Adam Cavanaugh since he had asked her out. The hotel grapevine had reported that he was in the building all week. She couldn't help but wonder why he hadn't come by just to say hello. But then this evening wasn't nearly as special to him as it was to her.

There were several reasons why tonight's date was significant. It was her first official date since her husband's accidental death. Her escort was a contemporary equivalent to Prince Charming. And it was a means by which to forget about the man who lived in the house behind hers. In a very short time, Thad Randolph had become a disturbing factor in her life.

She didn't like thinking about what had happened when she'd discovered him sick in his bedroom. She hated remembering what he looked like lying naked in that sexily rumpled bed. Each time she recalled him resting his cheek against her thigh, she ached with arousal. His parting words had been repeated in her head so many times, they should have lost their impact. They hadn't.

She had avoided even glancing toward his house the rest of the week, though she'd sent Matt and Megan over to check on him. They had reported back that he had made a remarkable recovery. So why couldn't she forget the incident and pretend that it hadn't happened?

That's what she tried to do each night when she retired to her bedroom and picked up her notebook and pen. Lilah had pestered her to write out more of her fantasies. So to satisfy her insatiable sister and to distract her own one-track mind, she had done just that. The only problem was that the imaginary men in her fantasies had begun to look like Thad. If anyone, these romantic figments of her imagination should have looked like Adam, who was much more classically handsome.

She had rearranged her characters' features and changed their hair colors so they would in no way resemble Thad, but in even the most recent fantasy, the rakehell pirate had looked like a younger version of him.

When the manicurist was finished with her, she led Elizabeth through the salon to the hair stylist who was waiting to comb her out. He removed the curlers, then surprised her by saying, "Throw your head forward." He combed her hair out upside down using only his fingers. When she tossed her head back, her light blond hair fanned out wide and wild around her head.

Well, it was different.

So different that when she returned home, her children gaped at her. "Gee, Mom, you look like one of the Solid Gold dancers."

"Oh, Lord," she said and moaned.

Before Mrs. Alder left, she informed Elizabeth that the lady from the dry cleaners had called to say that there was a slight problem with her dress. "What kind of problem?" she asked, thinking of cloth-eating chemicals.

"She didn't say, but I'm sure it's nothing earth-shattering. Have a good time."

It *was* earth-shattering. One of the cleaners' new employees had sent her only nice dress across town to another Mrs. Burke. They'd been trying to reach the woman by phone all afternoon, but hadn't succeeded. "I'm afraid that we might not get your dress to you until the first of next week."

When Elizabeth hung up, she was so dejected she decided to call Adam Cavanaugh, apologize profusely, and tell him that she couldn't make it for reasons beyond her control. Just as she was about to dial the Hotel Cavanaugh, the telephone rang.

"Hi, it's me," Lilah said cheerfully. "I made you three hundred and seventy-two dollars in sales this afternoon, but heaven I'm tired. Before I collapse with a glass of wine, I thought I'd call."

"Oh, Lilah." Elizabeth slumped into the nearest chair and told her about the dry cleaners' snafu. "I don't have anything else to wear that's appropriate."

"Well, if you ask me, this is the best thing that could have happened. That dress makes you look as old as Whistler's mother. I'll bring over something for you to wear."

"Out of *your* closet?"

"Well, you don't have to sound so horrified."

Lilah's hurt tone made Elizabeth feel rotten. "Your clothes look terrific on you. But our tastes don't coincide."

"I'll bring my dowdiest duds."

"Thanks a lot."

"Finally," Lilah said dramatically, "I've got you laughing. Don't worry. Everything will be fine. Do something relaxing until I get there."

She gave Megan and Matt permission to make "slice and bake" cookies while she went upstairs to take a soothing bubble bath. While partially reclining in the tub, she wrote out the pirate-captive fantasy she had daydreamed that afternoon. It was a cliché, but it was fun. Lilah would probably enjoy it even if it were never submitted for publication. She owed her sister a favor.

She smelled the burning cookies the minute she opened the bathroom door. Handwritten pages in hand, she raced down the stairs to rescue the sheet of charcoaled dough from the oven. Megan and Matt had become engrossed in a movie on TV and had forgotten to set the oven timer. While the three of them were fanning smoke out of the kitchen, Lilah arrived.

"Your hair looks great!" she cried the moment she stepped into the kitchen, carrying several garments over her arm. "You look like a Solid Gold dancer." The children laughed uproariously. Elizabeth rolled her eyes heavenward. "Did I say something funny?" Lilah asked.

"Not really." Elizabeth took her hand and dragged

her upstairs. "Let's see what outlandish outfits you've brought."

The differences in their coloring were so subtle one barely noticed them. But while Lilah could wear bright colors, they did nothing for Elizabeth but make her look sallow. From the dresses Lilah brought for her consideration, she selected a two-piece silk suit with a long pleated skirt. The one-button jacket had shoulder pads and a shawl collar that extended all the way to its hem. It was smart and dressy enough for dinner. The shade of pink was brighter than pastel, but didn't drain her complexion of all color.

She looked at herself from every angle in the cheval glass. "It'll go with the gray shoes I planned on wearing. Besides, I don't have much choice. Adam's due here in fifteen minutes," she said, consulting the clock on her dresser. "Which reminds me, where's the baby-sitter? She said she'd be here by seven."

"I'll check downstairs," Lilah said. "The kids might have already let her in."

Elizabeth finished dressing and, after giving herself one last hasty glance in the mirror, switched out her bedroom light and went downstairs. She could hear her family talking in the kitchen. When the doorbell rang as she was making her way across the living room, she was glad she was alone to answer the door. Her children might do something horrendous in front of Adam Cavanaugh, though she had demanded that they be on their best behavior when she introduced them.

Arranging her face into a welcoming smile and taking a restorative breath that did nothing to calm her jumpiness, she opened the front door. "What are you doing here?" she asked, saying the first thing that popped into her mind.

Thad was standing on her threshold holding a bouquet of roses wrapped in green tissue paper. He truly had made a remarkable recovery. If the man had ever been sick a day in his life, one couldn't tell it tonight. He was the picture of health and virility. Despite her rude question, his smile was wide and warm.

"I came to say thank you for being such a good neighbor when I was sick."

"Oh, that. Well, you're welcome."

An awkward silence ensued. The last time they had faced each other, she'd been wearing a nervous smile and he'd been wearing a sheet, and they both remembered what he'd said about finishing his dream.

"May I come in?"

"Of course." Before she closed the front door behind him, Elizabeth anxiously glanced up and down the street, but didn't see an approaching car. "My children will be glad to see you."

"I'm not here to see your children, Elizabeth."

His meaning couldn't be mistaken. If she had mistaken his meaning, the rapacious way he was looking at her would have clarified it. "The roses are beautiful," she said anxiously. "Are they for me?"

He extended the bouquet to her. "I didn't know if you liked roses."

"I love them."

"That color was so soft and feminine, it reminded me of you."

Self-consciously she sniffed the fragrant white blooms. The delicately ruffled edges of the petals were tipped with pink, as though they'd been kissed. "Thank you, Thad." She raised her head and caught him looking at her with puzzlement.

"Why are you all dressed up? Are you going out?"

"Well, yes, I—"

"Thad!"

"Thad!"

Megan and Matt barged through the swinging door that connected the dining room to the kitchen. Lilah followed. Her eyes rounded with surprise and amusement when she saw her sister talking with Thad. Elizabeth made awkward introductions while her children competed for Thad's attention with the fervency of pennant contenders.

"So pleased to meet you," Lilah cooed. "You brought roses! How thoughtful." She slid an inquiring glance toward her sister.

"I, uh, Thad was sick earlier in the week. He just dropped by to thank me for, for, uh . . ."

"Going into his house to check on him."

"Yeah, and she wouldn't let us go in to visit 'cause we might catch the flu."

"But she's a mom and can't catch the flu so she went in—"

"All by herself and—"

"He was in his bed—"

"And she did stuff for him—"

"And he got well."

The children's explanation was thorough, yet left holes as large as elephants for Lilah to fill with imagination. She gave her sister a speculative glance that said "Still waters run deep." Elizabeth prayed to be vaporized on the spot.

But since that didn't happen, she headed for the kitchen. "Excuse me. I need to get these roses in water."

"Oh, Lizzie, you've got a problem."

"Another one?"

"A major one. The baby-sitter isn't coming."

"What?"

"I hate to have to tell you, but her little brother

rode his bike over and said to tell you that she's got the flu."

"Must be going around," Thad said out of the corner of his mouth. He was still chuckling over the tale the children had told and their mother's embarrassed reaction to it.

Elizabeth wished he'd go home. Damn him! Why had he lived behind her all this time, but had chosen tonight of all nights to come calling with a bouquet of roses? While Lilah was here. When Adam was due to arrive any minute. She gnawed her lip in exasperation.

"I'll call Mrs. Alder." She turned toward the kitchen again, but, as before, was brought up short by Lilah.

"I already called her. She's sitting for someone else tonight."

"Do I smell something burning?" Thad asked blandly.

"The cookies!"

Lilah, Megan, and Matt all shrieked the word at the same time and stampeded back into the kitchen, with Thad and Elizabeth bringing up the rear. Acrid smoke was billowing out of the oven door.

"Lilah, how could you let this happen again?" Elizabeth wailed.

"You know I can't cook."

"Then why were you baking cookies?"

"To keep the kids occupied so they'd stay out of your way while you were getting dressed for your big date."

During this shouted exchange, Thad calmly removed the charred remains from the oven. "Big date?"

Through the cloud of smoke, his inquiring gaze found Elizabeth. Defensively she stuck out her chin. She didn't owe him any explanations, no matter how accusing his expression.

But the point was moot. There wasn't going to be a big date. "It's too late to start calling other baby-sitters," she said morosely. "I guess I can't go. Unless . . ." She looked at Lilah expectantly.

"Sorry, Lizzie, but I can't."

"Please, Lilah. I hate to impose on you twice in one day, but you know how important this evening is to me."

"It's not that I won't. I really can't. One of my former patients is having a birthday party. I promised to be there. It'll break her heart if I renege."

Elizabeth's shoulders slumped and she gave her sister a wan smile. For all Lilah's flamboyance, she was dedicated to her physical therapy patients. "By all means, you must go. Well, I guess that's—"

"I'll stay with the kids."

The words were softly spoken, but they had an impact on everyone in the kitchen. Lilah gave Thad an approving once-over. Elizabeth held his stare, her lips parting in surprise. The children rushed toward him, nearly knocking him down with their exuberance.

"That'll be neat, Thad."

"Can we give Baby a bath? Mom doesn't like for us to, 'cause it gets water all over the bathroom floor."

"Will you play games with us?"

"Can we stay up late?"

"Do you know how to make pizza?"

He responded to all their questions, but didn't take his eyes off Elizabeth.

Lilah stepped in, assuming the role of diplomat for the first time in her life. No one had to spell out to her that her sister and Thad Randolph needed a moment or two alone. "Come on, kids. I've got to get to my birthday party. Help me carry those clothes from upstairs."

"Are you gonna stay with us, Thad?" Megan asked hopefully.

"Yeah, I'm staying."

Matt and she whooped with glee before following their aunt Lilah from the room. Elizabeth and Thad continued to stare at each other. Finally she said, "Are you sure you don't mind, Thad?"

His eyes told her that he minded a helluva lot. Not staying with the children. But the idea of her going out on a "big date" didn't sit well with him. However, his voice was controlled when he said, "I owe you a favor, don't I?"

"I'll appreciate it very much."

He nodded, looking like a man who had a tenuous hold on his temper. "Go on." He hitched his head toward the upstairs. "Finish combing your hair so you'll be ready when he gets here."

"My hair is combed."

His jaw went slack. "It's supposed to look like that?"

The tangled curls shook with indignation. "It's got mousse and spritz on it."

"What's moosensprits?"

Before she could dress down his ignorance of hair fashion, the doorbell rang. "That'll be him." She spun around and shoved open the swinging door, wishing that Thad would have enough common courtesy to stay hidden in the kitchen. But if wishes came true, she wouldn't be in this predicament.

She answered the door on Adam's second ring. His broad smile was as guileless as the eye of a hurricane, which was apropos since he was the center of a storm and didn't even know it.

"Hello, Adam. Come in."

"Sorry I'm late. I missed the house the first time and had to drive around the block before—"

He broke off when he spotted Thad, who was leaning against the arched doorway of the dining room. Ankles crossed, arms casually folded across his chest, his air was that of a prospector who had staked the first claim. Up until fifteen minutes ago, he'd never set foot under her roof, but he looked well at home now.

Elizabeth cleared her throat uneasily as the two men appraised each other. "Adam, this is my neighbor, Thad Randolph."

Adam stepped forward. Thad indolently pushed himself away from the wall. They shook hands obligatorily.

"Thad's helping me out tonight with my children. My sitter canceled at the last minute, so . . ." Elizabeth shrugged, hoping her date got the gist of the situation and would fill in the blanks for himself.

"Oh, I see, well, good. Thanks, Randolph."

The smile that could melt a block of ice at twenty paces didn't faze Thad, who replied stonily, "You're welcome."

Adam extended Elizabeth a bouquet of roses. "These are for you."

She took them from him. "Thank you. They're . . . they're lovely."

At that moment, her children came charging down the stairs. Like cartoon characters they braked and stacked together when they saw that Adam Cavanaugh had arrived. They approached him with the appropriate deference. Elizabeth made the introductions.

"Hello, Mr. Cavanaugh," Megan said politely.

"Hello, Mr. Cavanaugh," Matt echoed.

Elizabeth breathed a profound sigh of relief. Her little darlings had come through.

"Those flowers are just like the ones Thad brought Mom. You must'a bought 'em at the same place."

"I could have killed him."

Now, it was easy to laugh at what Matt had said a few hours earlier. But when it had happened, it hadn't been very funny. Elizabeth had hoped the ground would open up and swallow her.

Adam smiled at her over their candlelit table. "I knew it made you uncomfortable, but I saw the humor in it." He twirled his brandy snifter. "Can't say the same for Mr. Randolph. He didn't crack a smile."

"Oh, don't mind him," Elizabeth said with a negligent wave of her hand. "Sometimes he comes across as being austere. Actually he's very nice. And great with my children."

"Only with your children?"

She lowered her eyes quickly. "We, Thad and I, are just good friends." And weren't they? Why, then, had she felt so guilty about being swept down the front walk to Adam's sleek foreign car parked at the curb and leaving Thad behind to baby-sit for her? There was no reason on earth why she should feel bad about it. He had volunteered to baby-sit, hadn't he? She hadn't twisted his arm.

Adam was enough of a gentleman to let the subject drop before it got too personal and signaled the hovering waiter to refill their coffee cups. Adam was a gentleman about everything. Elizabeth had feared that after such an inauspicious beginning, the evening would turn out to be a total disaster. She had to credit him with turning it around. He'd been affable and charming about the whole thing.

"I thought we'd check out the competition tonight," he had told her when they were en route to one of the city's posh restaurants. "I've thought about hiring this chef away from here and installing him in one of my hotels. Let's give him a secret audition."

Dinner had been a success. He had ordered the wine according to her entrée selection. The appetizers had been tasty, the sauces superb, the vegetables crisp, the dessert sumptuous. Adam directed the conversation to a variety of topics, which she also found interesting. He invited her to join him on the dance floor and they moved together well.

When he complimented her on her talent, she explained, "I took dancing until I graduated from high school. I loved it."

"What about your sister?"

The animosity that had crackled between Lilah and Adam the first time they met in Fantasy had rekindled when he noticed her coming down the stairs of Elizabeth's house. They had exchanged civil hellos, but their mutual dislike was palpable.

"Lilah didn't like dancing," Elizabeth told him now. "She was more into sports."

"Football and ice hockey, no doubt."

Elizabeth laughed. "Not quite. Tennis, softball, track. She was always more competitive than I, and somewhat of a tomboy."

"That I can believe," he had said under his breath as he led her back to their table.

Now, as they finished their coffee, Elizabeth wondered how this relaxed evening would end. She didn't have long to wonder. While they waited for the parking valet to bring his car around, Adam curled his hand around her upper arm.

"Is there any reason for you to rush home?"

Her insides had been warmed by the expensive vintage wine, the delicious food, the rich dessert. Her senses were pleasantly humming, like the strings of a violin beneath a gifted maestro's touch. Her escort was as handsome as a movie idol and was smiling at her with an unmistakable hint of intrigue. She felt beautiful, light-headed, and light-hearted. For once in her life, she longed to be reckless, to be swept headlong into a madcap love affair.

She found it easy to say, "No, Adam. I don't have to rush home. Why?"

"Have you ever seen the penthouse I use when I'm in town?"

She swallowed hard and answered huskily. "No."

"Would you like to?"

Eight

"Thank you again, Adam. I had a wonderful time."

"The pleasure was mine. Good night, Elizabeth. I'll see you soon."

He brushed his lips across her forehead. She gave him one last smile, then slipped through the front door of her house. The living room was dark. She took several groping footsteps toward the nearest lamp, but before she found it, Thad's voice lurched at her from out of the darkness.

"Have a good time?"

"Lord," she exclaimed, "you scared me to death." Switching on the lamp, she found him sprawled in the corner of her sofa. He'd taken off his boots; they were on the floor. The sport coat he'd had on earlier in the evening was lying across the arm of the easy chair. His shirt was still tucked in, but barely, and it was unbuttoned to his waist.

"Have a good time?" he repeated through lips that barely moved.

Idle curiosity hadn't prompted him to ask. Not even polite interest. His voice was only a hair breadth above a growl. In her present mood, Elizabeth took offense. Her ego had been bruised, but she would be damned before she'd let him know it. Not that her personal life was any of his business in the first place.

Flashing him a dazzling smile, she said, "I had a marvelous time." For emphasis, she executed a delightful little shiver which won her his glower. "What are you doing sitting in the dark?"

"What's wrong with the dark?"

"Nothing. But why aren't you in the den watching TV?"

"I didn't feel like it."

At the moment she didn't like him very much. She took exception to his casual slouching on her sofa, and to his open shirt, but especially to what was resting on his flat stomach. A highball glass.

He caught the direction of her gaze and tilted the glass toward her in a mocking salute. "Care to join me in a nightcap?"

"No."

"I hope you don't mind that I helped myself."

She did mind. Not that he had poured himself a drink from her small stock of liquor. What she minded was that he wasn't being his normal, nice self. He was being as surly as a street thug. And why? Was he regretting having baby-sat for her? What she minded most, however, was that he was still attractive in spite of his belligerence. Maybe even more so.

She tossed her purse down on the hassock in front of the chair. "No, I don't mind that you helped yourself to a drink. Did the children give you any trouble?"

"None at all. Did you give Cavanaugh any?"

She glared right back at his censorious blue eyes. "I don't like your tone of voice, Thad."

He rolled off his spine into a sitting position and placed his glass on the coffee table with a solid thud. His shirt fell open, revealing that muscled, hairy chest that she was trying to keep her eyes away from. "Well, that's just too damn bad, Elizabeth. Because this is the tone you're gonna get tonight."

"Wrong. I'm not going to listen to you at all." She drew herself up straight. "I appreciate the favor you did for me tonight. Thank you. Now I think you'd better leave."

Reaching the front door and dismissively holding it open for him was her goal. She never achieved it. No sooner had she given him her back, than he sprang off the couch as lithely as a panther and grabbed her upper arm. He spun her around to face him.

"Do you know what time it is?"

His rough treatment stunned her, so for a moment, the question seemed out of context. But then it dawned on her that it was rife with nasty implications. "Close to one-thirty, I believe," she replied sweetly. "Why? Is your wristwatch broken?"

His jaw knotted with fury and a muscle in his cheek twitched dangerously. "Why are you coming home so late? What were you doing all that time with Cavanaugh?"

"Having dinner."

"For six damn hours?"

"Be quiet. You'll wake up the children."

He lowered his voice, but repeated his words in an accusing hiss. "I never had a meal that took six hours to eat."

"After dinner we went dancing." One dance around a postage-stamp-sized dance floor hardly constituted "dancing," but out of sheer spite, she wanted Thad to think that Adam and she had cut a swath of gaiety through the city's nightclubs.

He sneered. "Dancing?"

"Yes, dancing. Adam likes to dance as much as I do."

"And after that what did you do? Where did you go?" Deliberately she lowered her eyes, trying her best to look discomfited by the question. "You went to his room, didn't you?"

"*Room?* Ha! That word falls short of describing the penthouse on the top floor of the Hotel Cavanaugh."

The taut skin across his cheekbones stretched even tighter. His eyes were cold with rage, yet hot with jealousy. They narrowed on her face as he said sibilantly, "You slept with him."

She wrested her arm free. "You are my neighbor, Thad, and up until a few minutes ago, I thought you were my friend. You have *never* been my father confessor." She drew a shaky breath. "Now kindly leave my house."

She didn't even wait to see him out. After picking up her purse, she turned her back on him and marched upstairs. She tiptoed into each child's bedroom and was relieved to see that they had slept through the shouting match.

The instant she entered her bedroom, she caught a glimpse of herself in the mirror and noticed how rosy her cheeks were. Thad's accusation hadn't brought color to her cheeks because it was so close to the truth, but because it was so far from it.

She stepped out of her shoes and took off Lilah's suit. She hung it on its padded hanger, placed it in her closet, and finished undressing. After dropping her nightgown over her head, she moved to her dressing table and gazed at her reflection. She said to it, "You're quite a siren, Elizabeth Burke."

Her nightgown matched her mores; it, too, was from another era. Made of white cotton, it had a wide scooping neckline and sleeves that ended in gathered ruffles at her wrists. There was a deep eyelet flounce on the skirt. Old-fashioned and quaint . . . just like her, or so everyone apparently thought.

Smiling wryly, she picked up her hairbrush and used it to destroy the thirty-dollar hairdo that was so out of character. As she did so, she began laughing softly to herself, recalling how her feet had floated over the carpeted floor from the private elevator to the etched glass doors of the penthouse.

She had been thinking that at last she was going to live one of her fantasies. She'd been a virgin when she married John Burke. He was the only man she'd ever slept with. Even her own sister would find that hard to believe, but it was true.

Tonight, she had thought, why not join the rest of the human race? Why not take an opportunity when it was offered? No exercizing sound judgment. No consideration for the consequences. Just going with the flow. Just enjoying a sexual encounter for no reason beyond the physical pleasure it would bring. "Good-bye to Sandra Dee." Isn't that how the song went?

Sandra Dee was tedious. Elizabeth was ready to be the bad girl for a change. They had all the fun. She was sick of being Miss Goodie Two Shoes because Miss Goodie Two Shoes was dull, dull, dull. Every day she handled merchandise that catered to romance, but it was always for someone else's romance, never her own.

The only time she ever shed her inhibitions and her stifling cloak of morality was in her fantasies. As a result, life was passing her by. The years would slip away. She couldn't think of a more pathetic picture than that of an old lady lost in her fantasy world and having nothing else to sustain her, not even bittersweet memories of actual love affairs.

So when Adam Cavanaugh had opened the doors of the penthouse and ushered her inside, she had virtually drifted in, willing to taste the forbidden fruit of modern sexuality.

But the joke had been on her.

Adam had been passionate, all right. Passionately excited . . . about the new hotel he was building in Chicago. He had led her into the bedroom, his eyes sparkling with promise . . . to show her the scale model of the new hotel. His voice had trembled with desire . . . to see this model become a reality. He'd been orgasmic . . . about what this latest addition could mean to his fleet of hotels. Afterward, they had talked shop over Danish and coffee which he'd had room service bring up.

Smiling wistfully over her own naïveté, Elizabeth laid her hairbrush down and turned away from the mirror. As she did so, there was a soft tap on her door. "Come in, darling," she said.

Thad Randolph stepped across her bedroom threshold and closed the door behind him. The latch clicked shut. Elizabeth stared at him, aghast.

"Who were you expecting? Cavanaugh?"

Rapidly recovering from her shock, she snapped, "Actually, I was expecting one of my children. I didn't think you'd be rude enough to go creeping through my house in the middle of the night, especially after I ordered you to leave."

"I hadn't said everything I wanted to say."

"Well, I'd heard everything I wanted to hear."

"Like how irresponsible you're being? I would have expected more out of a woman like you."

"Expected more of what? And what do you mean,

'a woman like' me? What sets me apart from every other woman?"

"Discretion. Decency. And intelligence. You know that Adam Cavanaugh is a playboy, don't you? You have no business messing with a smooth operator like him."

"He's not a smooth operator. He's a gentleman in every sense of the word."

He advanced into the room. Elizabeth got the impression that he was keeping his voice low only for the sake of the sleeping children whose rooms were at the opposite end of the hall. She also detected the smell of liquor on his breath. Apparently he'd spent his time downstairs fueling his anger with another drink.

"If he acted like a gentleman, it was only because he knew that's what he'd have to be to get you in his bed. But the only thing that separates him from the sharks who cruise the streets picking up girls is the price of his suit. Or is that what has you so starry-eyed? His money?"

"Absolutely not! I like him. He's interesting and—" It suddenly occurred to her that she didn't have to justify anything she did to Thad Randolph. One arranged date to an elementary-school Fall Festival was hardly tantamount to posting banns. She placed her hands on her hips. "What gives you the right to cross-examine me, Mr. Randolph?" Then, assuming the provocative posture of a coquette, she angled her head to one side and batted her eyelashes Southern-belle style. "Or are you concerned for my virtue? Are you lecturing me for my own good?"

She had never heard spoken aloud the word he said then. It singed her ears. The vulgar expletive was particularly paralyzing coming from soft-spoken, kind Mr. Randolph. That's why she was rooted to the floor with amazement when he lunged forward and caught her shoulders between his hands, shaking her slightly.

"Dammit, Elizabeth, you wouldn't know what was good for you if it walked right up and . . . and . . . oh, hell."

His mouth came down hard. It was a fiery, possessive, savage kiss that enraged her. She raised her hands to his chest and disconcertingly encountered bare skin. Despite the initial shock, she gave a mighty push.

But he wouldn't be budged. Nor would he be denied. When she tore her lips free of his and tried to avert her head, he sank all ten fingers into her hair and held her head a helpless, immovable captive between his strong hands.

"Kiss me back, damn you."

He thrust his tongue into her mouth, swiftly and surely. The violation was so absolute, so irrevocable, that it was like experiencing the breach of virginity all over again. Reflexively she arched against him. Her fingers curled inward, but barely dented the solid muscles beneath them. Her nightgown was sheer, a negligible shield against his virility. All his anger and frustration seemed to be concentrated in his thighs and lower body. They were rock-hard and unyielding as they pressed into her softness.

But more distressing than his possessiveness was her reaction to it. A wildfire of sensation radiated from the tops of her thighs to the tips of her extremities. She struggled against this involuntary response. "Stop this, please, Thad."

His answer was to sweep her up into his arms and carry her to the bed, where he unceremoniously tossed her down. This reversal of his benign personality astounded her so much she couldn't move.

She lay there and stared up at him with incredulity as he angrily shoved off his shirt and went for his belt buckle.

"What are you doing?"

"That should be obvious." He unbuckled his belt and unzipped his pants, but didn't remove them. Instead he sauntered toward the bed. Fighting the urge to stare at the wedge of dark hair his open trousers had exposed, Elizabeth shrank from him and cowered against the headboard. Grinning triumphantly, he reached down, grasped her wrist, and hauled her to her feet so abruptly that her teeth clicked together.

He planted the heels of his hands at the small of her back, curved his fingers down over her derriere, and jerked her against him. Lowering his head, his mouth sought her evasive lips once again. When she failed to comply to his silent demands, he brought one hand around and squeezed her jaw between his fingers. His lips forced hers apart.

She moaned, first in outrage, then in helpless surrender, as his tongue slid in and out of her mouth in so sexual a cadence she felt her bones melting.

He recognized her capitulation within a heartbeat. His tongue ceased to be a plunderer and became a lover, stroking her mouth to ecstasy. By slow degrees, her struggles ceased, her body relaxed and became pliant, molding itself to his, reshaping itself to fit his steely contours.

"Elizabeth." He groaned. "Dear Lord, Elizabeth."

His open mouth moved down her neck. His hand searched for and found the buttons on her gown, but they stubbornly refused to come undone. Arousal gave him superior strength, which the daintily tucked and pleated bodice couldn't withstand. The sound of tearing cloth joined that of their ragged breathing. The nightgown dropped to the floor, creating a puff of air when it landed around her ankles.

His parted lips followed the curve of her breast. Then he lifted his head and visually devoured her nakedness. He cupped one breast in his hand and played with the dusky crest until it became stiff. Growling with gratification, he ducked his head and whisked it with his tongue, again and again, until Elizabeth clung to him for support.

He swept her into his arms. Only this time, when he deposited her onto the bed, he did so with gentleness. His eyes were alight with passion, not anger. His face was taut with desire, not enmity.

She stared up at him with wide-eyed misapprehension as he backed off the bed and removed his trousers and a pair of jockey briefs. When he lay down beside her, he was naked. And warm. And hairy. And manly. And wonderful.

He raised her hand to his lips and kissed the palm, then carried it down to his sex. He acquainted her with the dimension, the power and strength, of his desire for her. "This gives me the right to ask, to *know*. Did you sleep with Cavanaugh tonight, Elizabeth?"

"No. Of course I didn't."

He stared deeply into her eyes, searching for signs of mendacity, but saw only leaping arcs of desire. He impressed a hungry, twisting kiss on her receptive mouth. His sex became even fuller within her caressing grasp. He nudged her knees apart and settled himself heavily within the cradle of her thighs.

In one long, slow plunge, he imbedded himself between the stretching walls of her body. Elizabeth, thrilled with his magnificent strength, brought her knees up to accommodate him. He moaned with supreme satisfaction and buried his face in the perfumed cloud of her hair which was spread out on the pillow.

Though it seemed impossible, he delved deeper into her with each rhythmic push. She felt those supple contractions against her hands which greedily drew him closer, higher. He kissed her ears, her throat, and, as his thrusts accelerated, her mouth.

After several moments she clasped his head and held it away from her. Her breath was choppy; her flushed breasts rose and fell with each shallow pant. "You don't have to wait on me, Thad."

He looked surprised, then smiled tenderly. "Yes I do."

"No, really. You don't have to do that for me."

"I'm not," he said hoarsely. "I'm doing it for me."

She gave a joyful little gasp when he slid his splayed hands beneath her hips. He rubbed his face against her nipples, once, twice, letting her feel his cheeks, chin, nose, and tongue against them.

With his next deep thrust, her neck involuntarily arched and she lost herself in this splendid mating rite. Her hips responded to his clenching fingers. She ground her body against his, wanting more, always more.

And when she was seized by a rush of sensation so intense she couldn't contain it, she bit her lower lip to hold back a scream of pleasure. The immensity of it was compounded when she felt, deep inside her, the staccato spasms of his release.

Neither knew if it was seconds, minutes, or eons that they lay in a state of complete exhaustion. Thad was the first to move. He propped himself on one elbow and gazed down at her.

"You're beautiful," he said, still breathing unevenly.

"You think so?"

"Oh, yeah," he drawled, smiling and nodding his head.

His unhurried caresses matched his inflection. He drew his index finger across her chin, down her throat, and then continued across her collarbone. From there it meandered over her breasts, following the high curves and dipping into the shallow valley between them. He traced a faint white stretch mark.

"I've been a mother twice," she reminded him apologetically.

He only growled with pleasure. "You certainly have."

Leisurely he circled each nipple with the tip of his finger until they both responded prettily. Lowering his mouth to one, he flicked it with his tongue, then closed his lips around it and sucked gently. Elizabeth made a whimpering sound.

"You like that?" he asked, moving his lips over the glistening bead of flesh.

"Yes."

"Good. So do I. Very much." He covered her other nipple with his mouth and tugged at it hard enough to give pleasure, but temperate enough to prevent pain. He raked his teeth against it and plucked at it lightly with his lips. "I was dreaming of this when you woke me up the other day. I was making love to your sweet breasts."

"You said as much."

"I've had some wonderful dreams about you lately, but you never felt this good against my tongue in any of them. And nothing I've ever dreamed of tasted as good as this."

She had thought that John Burke was a romantic man. But compared to her late husband, Thad was Cyrano de Bergerac. He had the soul of a poet, but the carnal appetites of a sultan.

"You're quite a lover, aren't you, Thad?"

He raised his eyes to hers, at first thinking that she was teasing. But when he saw that she was serious, he answered in kind. "I've had very few complaints from the women I've been with."

"And how many is that?" Regretting the words the moment they were out, she turned her head into the pillow. "I'm sorry. Forget I said that. I have no right to ask."

After a lengthy pause, he said softly, "I bought the teddy for you." Her head came around and she stared up at him, speechless with surprise. "That's right. For you. There is no other woman right now." He reshaped the underside of her breast to fit his hand and fondled her as he spoke. "When I got back from Vietnam, my fiancée ditched me for another guy. Actually, she had ditched me long before I got back, but she was kind enough not to write and tell me so.

"Since then, I've kept my relationships brief. I took what I wanted from them, gave back only enough to salve my conscience, then split while lust was the only thing the woman and I had in common. I'm not a saint. Never pretended to be. So, yes, I've been with a lot of women.

"But I never allowed myself to focus on any one woman because, frankly, I liked being single. And," he added, with a shrug, "I guess maybe I was afraid to fall in love and be jilted again. Anyway, I liked my life the way it was.

"Then I moved here. Your kids were so damn cute, I began to have second thoughts about my lifestyle. Every now and then I got a hankering to have kids of my own.

He drew a deep sigh. "And then, of course, there was you. I'd catch myself peering through trees more often than not when I heard your car pull into the driveway. Whenever you came into the backyard I made up reasons to be outside myself just to get a glimpse of you, to see if you were as pretty as you looked from a distance. But you never initiated a conversation, so I left things alone. When I got lonely, I told myself that I was lucky and damn clever to remain unentangled.

"I thank providence for stranding that kitten up in the tree. It gave me a reason to come close." He ran his finger down her cheek. "The instant I looked into your face, the top of my head blew off. And every time I've seen you since then, I've wanted to be in bed with you, doing this."

His voice lowered to a seductive pitch. "That night I caught you by the water hydrant, I barely stopped myself from taking you against the wall."

"Why didn't you?"

He registered surprise. "Would you have let me?"

"I honestly don't know. Why didn't you at least try?"

His eyes looked turbulent, as though he were wrestling with the decision of whether or not to tell her. Finally he met her gaze squarely and said, "Because I thought then that I only wanted to have you sexually. And you deserved better than that."

Her gaze flickered away from his. His blunt honesty was unnerving. "So why did you come into the shop the next day?"

"I couldn't stay away. I wanted to get another look at you in the daylight, to convince myself that you were real. You were." He bent over her and planted a solid, hot kiss on her mouth. "Were you ever."

After another deep kiss he said, "So there I was in Fantasy, damn sure I wanted you, but unsure how you felt about me. I decided to test the waters by trying to make you jealous."

"That was a sneaky, rotten thing to do."

He smiled mischievously. "But it worked, didn't it?" She clamped her lips shut and refused to answer. "Come on, now. I made an ass of myself tonight when you came in from your date with Cavanaugh. Can't you admit to even a trace of jealousy?"

"All right, a trace. I thought it was extremely unchivalrous of you to come into my store to buy a scandalous piece of lingerie for your mistress."

"Mistress?" he echoed, laughing at the old-fashioned term. "Feel free to come over and slip into the teddy and stockings any time." He murmured the words against her throat. "They're still wrapped up in pink tissue paper, even though I've taken them out and played with them a few times."

"How perverted."

"Hmm. I imagined your breasts filling up those lace cups. Your nipples straining against them."

He kissed her thoroughly. His hand sawed back and forth in the hollow of her waist, then flattened against her stomach. He slid it down to cover the triangle of tawny hair. Elizabeth flushed with embarrassment when he ended their kiss so he could watch as his fingers explored. He let the pale curls ensnare them.

"So pretty," he whispered. "So soft and sexy."

And that was only the beginning.

"Is this . . . what you, uh, had in mind . . . when you put this . . . hmm . . . this hammock here?"

"Can you think of a better use for it?"

She sighed. "No."

Half an hour earlier he had said, "Walk me home."

She had thought the idea was crazy, but since she was reluctant for this night to end, she'd consented. She slipped on her ripped nightgown when he tossed it to her after retrieving it from the floor.

He'd stepped into his slacks . . . nothing else . . . and carried the rest of his clothes. They had crept out of the house, careful not to awaken the children, and left by way of the back door. Neither of them had noticed before how loudly its hinges squeaked until they pulled it open.

Laughing, and feeling wonderfully, naughtily adolescent, they had tiptoed across the cold, damp grass toward his house. Along the way, they stopped several times to kiss and caress. He had suggested that they try out the hammock he'd hung so well between the two trees. Elizabeth had made a bawdy crack about everything he had being well hung and he'd laughed and hugged her and told her she was an adorable, delightful contradiction.

So now they lay in the hammock. They should have been cold, but they weren't. Elizabeth was oblivious to the chill, even though the long skirt of her nightgown was bunched around her waist. She wasn't cold because Thad was lying on top of her . . . and inside her.

The arches of her feet, they had discovered, fit his calf muscles perfectly. That's where she rested them, when she wasn't reaching down to the ground to give the hammock a gentle push with the tips of her toes. The hammock's rocking motion was lazy, but heightened their sensations of each other a thousandfold.

"I didn't know you could— I mean, it's been— How can you stay—"

"Hard?" he asked. "How can I stay hard for so long?"

"Yes." She groaned as he pressed higher. "It's nothing short of a miracle."

"It's nothing short at all." He bobbed his eyebrows and grinned devilishly.

She laughed. The delicious vibration caused him to wince with pleasure. "We've been here for . . . what? Ten minutes?"

"Yeah, but that's nothing," he told her around a kiss. "I've been hard for almost two weeks."

"What?"

"Ever since I put my hands around your waist and lifted you out of that tree. The top of my head wasn't the only thing that nearly blew off."

"My composure slipped too. Even though you treated me with the respect befitting a neighbor widow lady. Nothing at all like the furious man who almost raped me tonight."

"Admittedly, I was furious. I didn't hurt you, did I?"

"No," she replied, touched by his concern. "I wasn't afraid you'd hurt me. But I didn't know you could be so aggressive."

"Only when sorely provoked and slightly drunk."

"Why were you sorely provoked and slightly drunk?"

"Because I couldn't stand the thought of you doing this with Cavanaugh. With anybody but me."

His honesty disarmed her. "Are you always so candid?"

"To a fault."

"I'm glad you don't play games. I admire straightforwardness."

His eyes turned dark with renewed desire. "Do you?"

"Yes."

"So if I wanted something," he said huskily, "you'd rather I come right out and ask instead of beat around the bush?" He dusted her lips with his.

Her heartbeat speeded up with excitement. "Yes."

"Lower the top of your nightgown," he whispered.

She hesitated for only a moment, then slowly raised

one hand to the lacy, elastic edge. Her breast swelled creamy and smooth above it as she gradually pulled it down. Thad groaned when the lace skimmed her nipple, caught on it, and drew it even more erect. At last her entire breast was revealed and she made to withdraw her hand.

"No, leave it there. Right there. Oh, Lord."

Staring fixedly at her hand and the idle movements of her fingers, he began to lightly grind his body into hers. Then not so lightly. The rotations quickened and her hips rose to meet them. Seconds later it ended in a frenzy of simultaneous explosions.

It took a long time for them to garner enough energy to leave the hammock and walk to his back porch. Holding the screen door open, he leaned out for one last, lingering kiss during which his tongue made sweeping, swirling motions inside her mouth. "I wish I could sleep with you," he said when they finally drew apart.

"So do I."

"Let me."

"I don't want the neighbors to see you sneaking out of my house at daybreak. Or let my kids find you in bed with me in the morning."

"No, I guess not."

"Please understand, Thad."

"I do." He lifted her hand to his mouth and kissed it. "But I'm inviting myself to breakfast. What time should I be there?"

Nine

They looked innocent enough when Matt and Megan stumbled sleepy-eyed into the kitchen and found them sitting together at the table and staring into each other's eyes over forgotten cups of coffee.

"Did Thad spend the night here?"

For all their subterfuge, that was the first thing Matt said. To the childrens' puzzlement, Thad and their mother burst out laughing.

"No, I didn't spend the night," he said. "It just looks that way to you. Your Mom invited me for breakfast." ·

"Funny, I thought you invited yourself," Elizabeth said to him out of the corner of her mouth as she rose to pour the children their ritual glasses of orange juice. He swatted her on the fanny, something that the kids thought was hilarious.

"Did Thad tell you about Baby's bath?" Megan asked. Elizabeth shook her head no. "He let us give her a bath. Cats don't like water, did you know that, Mom? But we bathed her anyway. She got real clean and fluffy, but we kinda made a mess."

"Only, Thad helped us clean it up or— What is it, Thad? Like in the army?"

"Police the area," Thad supplied.

"Yeah, we policed the area. Didn't he tell you, Mom?"

"No, he failed to mention that." She cast the man, who looked wonderfully good and right sitting at her breakfast table, a sidelong glance.

"As I recall, we had better things to talk about." He looked at her meaningfully and she grew warm beneath his gaze.

"And he let us order a pizza over the phone from the man who brings it to your house."

"Yeah, we told Thad that you said that kind of pizza was junk."

"But he said that you weren't here and so he was in charge and he *liked* that kind of pizza."

"Can we call the pizza man again, Mom? It wasn't junk, honest."

Placing her hands on her hips, Elizabeth faced Thad. "Thanks a lot. In a few hours you undid years of nutritional indoctrination."

He seemed supremely concerned. "What's for breakfast?"

"Curds and whey," she replied flippantly.

The children shrieked with laughter. To help calm them down, Thad supervised them setting the table while Elizabeth cooked the food.

"Hey, everybody here has to pull KP," Thad called to the children as they headed for the television set in the den as soon as they had finished eating. They didn't give him the argument they usually gave Elizabeth. She watched, her mouth agape, as they obediently returned to the table and cleared their own place settings, carrying the dirty dishes to the sink.

"How'd you do that?" she asked.

"Bribes." He took two packs of chewing gum out of his shirt pocket. "Sugar-free," he told Elizabeth before handing a package of gum to each child. They dutifully said thank you, which endeared them to their mother.

"And what does the cook get?"

"The cook gets a kiss."

Megan and Matt came to an abrupt halt on their way to the door and, as one, turned around in time to see Thad encircling their mother's waist with his arms. He angled his head to one side and kissed her on the mouth.

"Thad's kissing Mom!" Megan exclaimed.

"Ooh, gross!" That from Matt.

As soon as Thad and Elizabeth drew apart, the children started circling them like the attacking Indians around a wagon train. They whooped and hollered and flailed their arms wildly. Relieved and pleased that the two children were so enthusiastic about this sudden turn of events, Thad and Elizabeth started laughing at their antics, which only egged them on.

As usual, Matt's excitement got out of control. The harder Thad and his mother laughed, the more animated he became until on one unbalanced pivot, he crashed into the china cabinet. All the dishes rattled. A wooden bowl of fruit was overturned. Apples and oranges rolled in every direction. A tomato splattered onto the tile floor. Several sheets of notebook paper went flying about like chicken feathers before drifting down one by one.

Matt froze, and glanced up at his mother apprehensively. "I didn't mean to."

"You're such a dork," Megan said, now acting much older and much more superior.

Matt dropped to his knees. He avoided the globs of

tomato, but collected the scattered sheets of paper and carried them like a peace offering to Elizabeth. "Here, Mom. Your papers didn't get dirty. We didn't get pizza juice on them either. Thad moved them off the table and put them on the cabinet so they wouldn't get messed up. He said they might be important."

Elizabeth accepted the handwritten sheets from her son, who began crawling around on the floor, picking up the pieces of fruit.

"Just leave them, Matt." Elizabeth's voice was as thin and tight as a rubber band that had been stretched to its limit. "I'll clean up later. You and Megan please go upstairs and make your beds."

With the keen perception of children, they sensed that the mood in the room had drastically shifted and it wasn't because of Matt's accident. Something beyond their understanding had happened; it had made their mother's face go from rosy and smiling to pale and haggard. Her laughing lips were now drawn into a narrow line that barely moved when she spoke. Together, they left by way of the swinging door, making as little commotion as possible. They feared that something hung precariously in the balance and they didn't want to be the ones to upset it.

Elizabeth meticulously straightened and put the sheets of paper in numerical order before blinking the written words into focus. She knew what they were, of course. She'd written them while soaking in a bubble bath. Every phrase was familiar.

There was her pirate, tall and dangerous. There was his captive, shivering before him, wearing nothing but a thin nightgown. She rifled through the pages. Yes, there was the part where he ripped her nightgown and kissed her breast. And there, in that paragraph, the captive, overpowered by his masculine charm, began to submit and respond.

She tossed the pages onto the kitchen table and turned her back quickly. Folding her arms over her middle, she rubbed her forearms, though the kitchen was sufficiently warm for an autumn morning.

"You read it, didn't you?"

"Listen, Elizabeth, I—"

She spun around. *"Didn't you?"*

Thad's chest rose and fell with a heavy sigh. "Yes."

Tears filled her eyes. One instant the hot, salty products of humiliation weren't there, the next instant, her vision was blurred with them. She covered her chalky lips with a cold, trembling hand and turned away from him again. She couldn't bear to look him in the face, because of her embarrassment, because of his deceit. She didn't know which caused her the most pain.

In a quiet, soothing voice, the kind doctors use to break the bad news to the family, he said, "I didn't realize what it was at first. I thought you had left an unfinished letter lying around. But then a few words just leaped off the pages at me."

She faced him, her expression scornful. " 'Leaped off the pages'? Can't you do any better than that?"

He had the grace to look chagrined. "Haven't you ever thumbed through a novel in a bookstore, and when a certain word catches your eye, you stop and read a few paragraphs. And if it's a sensual passage, you keep on reading. Before you know it, you've devoured five or six pages standing there in the aisle. If that's never happened to you, you aren't normal."

"We're not talking about me. We're talking about an underhanded manipulator who used me in the lowest, meanest, most disgusting way possible. How *could* you?"

"I didn't do anything you didn't want me to."

She clenched her fists and squeezed her eyes shut. "I *knew* something dreadful would come of this. I never should have listened to Lilah, never let her talk me into this."

He looked confused. "Lilah talked you into dreaming up the story?"

"Into writing it down. She's submitting my fantasies to a publisher."

"Then why are you so ashamed of it? I read it and thought it was damn good."

She opened her eyes and glared at him. Anger had deepened the color of her eyes almost to the piercing hue of his. "Yes, you read it and turned it to your advantage. Why didn't I realize what was going on when you tore my nightgown? It was so out of character for you. You're not like that."

"How do you know?" he challenged. "We'd never made love before. And I was jealous enough and mad enough and drunk enough to get a little rough." He stepped forward and lowered his voice to a sexy growl. "And you liked it."

She backed away from him in revulsion. "Last night you told me that you thought I deserved better than just—" She couldn't bring herself to say the words.

"Apparently after reading my fantasy you changed your mind. I became fair game. After reading that," she said, gesturing down at the manuscript, "you must have thought I was pining for a flesh-and-blood lover. Or did you imagine that I must have a lot of them? Didn't the fantasy convert you from Good Neighbor Sam to Jean Lafitte because you thought that's what I wanted?"

"No. That's not what happened at all. Everybody has an alter ego, Elizabeth. Probably several of them. Yours surfaces in your fantasies. Mine surfaced last night. I wasn't even thinking about the damn fantasy when I came into your bedroom."

"Oh, please." She groaned with sarcastic disbelief. "You acted it out word for word!"

"Subconsciously maybe. I was an angry, jealous man responding to the woman I wanted like hell to take to bed. Reading your fantasy turned me on, yes. But it also made me crazy. I saw Cavanaugh in the pirate's role. Everything you described in such arousing detail, I imagined you doing with him."

"Well, I didn't. Because he's not a sneak and a liar and—" Another horrible thought occurred to her. "Is this the only one you've read?" He looked at her with a bewilderment too profound not to be phony. "It isn't, is it? You read the one about the pilot and the farm girl, didn't you? That's why when I came in and found you sick—"

She clapped her hands to her burning cheeks, just now fully realizing the implications. His interest in her coincided with when she first started writing down her fantasies. She always discarded her first drafts. "What have you been doing, scavenging the trash can every morning like an alley cat, looking for fresh material?"

How many handwritten drafts had she thrown away? How many had he enjoyed, snickering as he read each sensuous paragraph? "I'm amazed that you came up with the idea of the hammock on your own. I hadn't written a fantasy about that yet."

He propped his hands on his hips and assumed that arrogant, aggravated male stance. Elizabeth despised it because it strongly suggested that she was being incredibly stupid and unreasonable.

"I haven't the faintest idea what you're talking about," he said. "What's that about a pilot? And my being sick? Do you think I faked a fever of one hundred point four?"

"I wouldn't put anything past you." She summoned all the animosity she felt for him and placed it behind her next words. "Leave my house."

He shook his head no. "I'm not leaving while you're angry. Not until we get this settled."

"It's settled. I don't want to see you, ever again. I'm not sure I can even tolerate your living in the house behind me."

"Just like that?" He snapped his fingers.

"Just like that."

"After last night?"

"Nothing that happened was real."

"Oh, it was real," he said with a short laugh. "And you've got the marks on your body to prove it."

She blushed, remembering the faint bruises she had discovered on her breasts and thighs while she was showering. An hour ago, she had gloried in them, equating them to an artist's signature on his masterpiece. Now she was ashamed to think of how his mouth had put them there.

"Look, Elizabeth," he said with diminishing patience, "I don't blame you for being angry. I don't even blame you for jumping to the wrong conclusion. I read something I shouldn't have. It was personal and private. I violated your privacy by reading it. But"—he paused for emphasis—"the only way it changed my opinion of you was to make you more fascinating."

She aimed a straight finger down at the sheets of paper on the table. "I'm not the kidnapped girl, any more than you're the pirate. She's a figment of my imagination. She's nobody. She's make-believe."

He disputed her words with a slow, negative shake of his head. "She *is* you. She's what you secretly think, how you feel about sexuality, how you feel about love, what you want in bed but would never ask for. Just like the moon, we all have a dark side, a part of us that the world doesn't see. It's in our makeup and is nothing to be ashamed of."

He had backed her into the counter. She shook her head adamantly, fearfully. "I'm *not* like that."

"Not on the outside. On the outside, you're every inch a lady. Don't you realize that's what makes you so attractive, so damned fascinating?" His tone became softer, more cajoling. "Elizabeth, why do you think I wanted to sleep with you last night?"

His words about falling in love with a woman he liked waking up with came back to cruelly mock her now. She wouldn't believe him. She wouldn't be made a fool of again.

"So you could keep on using me until I finally caught on."

His brows drew together in an impatient frown. He braced his hands on either side of her hips and leaned over her, forcing her head back. "You're not angry because I read what you wrote. You wrote it to be read. You're upset because I'm not a stranger. You're not anonymous. Now I know your secret. Now I know that under your cool, prim exterior, you burn hot."

The words popped and hissed like drops of water on a hot skillet. Elizabeth's hand cracked across his cheek.

Neither could believe she'd slapped him. His eyes narrowed dangerously as he gradually pushed himself away from her and straightened up. She had spanked her children only on the rarest occasions, then cried harder than they afterward. The aggressive child in the family had been Lilah, never her older sister, who always gave in to avoid any chance of a physical altercation. But now she had slapped a man who easily outweighed her by seventy-five pounds and who towered over her.

The shock over striking him didn't alleviate her rage, however. She would never forgive him for the despicable way he'd manipulated her into making love with him. It made her sick to think that everything he'd said and done to her had come, not from his heart, but from a licentious curiosity.

She said nothing to detain him when he turned and angrily strode toward the door, nearly ripping it from its hinges when he opened it. What have you got to be so angry about? she wanted to shout at him. He'd gotten better than he deserved!

But she said nothing. Her voice box wouldn't function. It was too congested with emotion. She sank into the nearest chair, laid her head on the kitchen table, and submitted to the luxury of heart-rending sobs.

Things didn't improve with time.

For the next several days, her mood was funereal. She was so short-tempered with her children that they counterattacked by behaving their worst. One afternoon she caught them playing on Thad's hammock with the puppies, and yelled for them to come in right that minute. They set up a howl, asking her why they had to come in. She could provide no plausible answer. They sulked for the rest of the evening. When Megan told her she wished they lived with somebody fun like Thad, Elizabeth banished her to her room.

Lilah called to ask her about her date with Adam

Cavanaugh. Elizabeth was barely civil, unfairly blaming her sister for all her recent misfortunes.

"Gee," Lilah had said after several attempts to draw Elizabeth out, "you're a barrel of laughs. I'll call back when you're acting human."

Her foul disposition had successfully alienated her from everyone in her life. For a while that was fine. She didn't feel like talking to anybody. She nursed her misery like a witch did her brew, adding particles of resentment to it daily, stirring it, watching it simmer.

But gradually she disliked her solitude even more than she did other peoples' company. She was even glad to see Adam Cavanaugh when he came breezing through the door of her shop late one morning.

After calling her name twice, he laughed at her startled expression. "I always seem to catch you lost in thought. Where do you go when you leave the rest of us behind?"

She tried to recover quickly. She hadn't seen him since he'd walked her to her door and given her a discreet kiss on the forehead. He didn't take advantage of women the way *some* men did. And Thad had accused Adam of being a playboy!

"Daydreaming is a bad habit I picked up in childhood," she told him. "I'm a professional woolgatherer. My sister torments me about it."

At the mention of her sister, he frowned. "How is that disrespectful sister of yours?"

"Disrespectful," Elizabeth replied, thinking that it was time for her to mend her fences with Lilah. It wasn't Lilah's fault that Thad Randolph had turned out to be a rat.

"Lunch?" Adam asked, snapping her out of her thoughts.

"Lunch? Uh, no, thank you, Adam. I don't have

anyone to mind the shop if I go out. I usually brown-bag it here."

"Close for an hour. Please. I've been giving our evening together a lot of thought." His voice took on a mysterious pitch and his brown eyes danced with secrecy. "There's something very important I want to discuss with you."

Half an hour later, Elizabeth was picking at a salad she had built from the Garden Room's noon buffet. Adam and she were sitting at a corner table where two glass walls intersected to provide a great view of the city's skyline.

"Well?"

"I don't know, Adam. You've taken me completely off guard."

"You can't be too surprised by my proposal."

"But I am." She lifted troubled china-blue eyes to his inquiring ones. "I've never considered opening another Fantasy. This one takes so much time and energy."

"I can appreciate that," he said, after taking a sip of his iced water. "I took your situation into consideration. I realize that being a widow with two children isn't exactly conducive to owning and operating businesses in several cities at the same time. But I'm confident you can handle it."

Though the idea of opening several more Fantasy shops had come as a complete surprise, she was flattered. In spite of her myriad reservations, the idea had piqued an ambitious streak she hadn't known she had.

Leaning forward in his chair, Adam stressed his point. "Fantasy is the biggest money-maker, percent-agewise, of any of our lessees. That impresses me. *You* impress me. I can't find a single fault with you. Other than a little daydreaming," he teased. "You've tapped into a unique market. You buy intuitively. People will pay a quality price for a quality product. And the demographics show that the people who stay at my hotels are accustomed to doing everything first class."

"But I—"

He held up both hands to forestall her. "I'm saving a space for you in the lobby of the new Hotel Cavanaugh Chicago. Soon, I want to install your shops in other cities."

He went on to outline the feasibility of the proposal until Elizabeth developed a headache and begged him to stop and give her time to think.

"I deliberate for hours over whether to have tacos or pork chops for dinner," she told him, laughing. "I hope you don't expect an answer today."

"Of course not. Tomorrow will be soon enough."

Her face went blank with shock, but relaxed when she saw that he was joking. "No, I don't expect an immediate answer. Time's on my side. The longer you think about it, the better you're going to like the idea," he said confidently.

At the door of Fantasy, he told her, "I'll send down a typewritten proposal. Look it over. Study the figures. I'll call for your answer in a week or so. In the meantime, don't hesitate to call me if you have any questions." He flipped a business card from his suit coat pocket. "The number on here is a direct, private line. Use it."

As usual, Adam left her feeling out of breath and drained of energy. She envied him his self-confidence and the purpose with which he moved through life. He seemed to know exactly what he wanted and didn't let anything stand in his way. She wished she could be that decisive. Did she want to remain a small-scale operation or expand?

Lord, what did she, a widow with two children and a broken heart, know about big business?

A broken heart?

Her thoughts came to a standstill. Like most times when someone stumbles over something, he goes back to see what had tripped him up. A broken heart. Yep, there they were. Those three words had gotten in the path of her thoughts and impeded them.

Her heart *was* broken. She was in love with Thad Randolph. He was in lust with her, just like all those other women he'd bedded.

How could she possibly think about expanding her business or what to cook for dinner or anything else when she couldn't sort out her feelings for him? There should be no sorting to do. The categories of her feelings should be black and white instead of this infernal gray. She couldn't even pinpoint the moment her anger had turned to anguish, her fury to despair.

She took an aspirin for her pounding headache.

Her mood was slightly lifted when she returned home to discover Lilah's car parked in her driveway. She entered her house and found her sister scooping ice cream into bowls for Matt and Megan.

"Mrs. Alder left and Aunt Lilah said we could have ice cream," Matt reported importantly. He was also sitting on his knees in his chair. Another no-no.

"Before dinner?" Elizabeth asked, vexed.

"You know, I always wondered why Mom made that such a cardinal rule," Lilah said, wagging the ice-cream scoop at her sister. "What difference does it make if you eat your dessert before or after the meal?"

"You're hopeless." Elizabeth moved toward her sister, who was licking ice cream off the scoop, a nasty habit she'd tried to break her children of.

"Does that vague smile mean that I'm forgiven for whatever sin I committed?"

Elizabeth embraced her. She'd never been able to stay mad at Lilah for long. "You're forgiven."

"Thank God! I'd already invited the kids out to dinner. It would have been an interminably long one if you weren't speaking to me. What'd I do, anyway?"

"You didn't do anything. What prompted this invitation to dinner?"

"That."

Lilah nodded down at an envelope which Elizabeth hadn't yet noticed. She recognized the logo on the letterhead. "That's . . . that's— They didn't!"

"They did. Enclosed in that envelope, which I took the liberty of opening, is a letter of acceptance for two of your stories to be published in their book *and* a check for five hundred dollars. Is that wonderful or what?"

"That's wonderful!" Elizabeth cried. "Now the kids can have new coats and boots and we won't have to eat tuna all winter. Is there any ice cream left for me?"

"Now I *know* I'm forgiven," Lilah said, and laughed.

When the children finished their ice cream, they were sent upstairs to change their clothes. "We'll have a 'grownups only' celebration tonight after the kids go to bed," Lilah said. "There's a bottle of champagne chilling in the fridge."

"Sounds great."

Lilah looked at her sister closely. According to Elizabeth's expression, nothing was "great." "Are you going to tell me about it, or do I have to wait until we go to summer camp? That's when you imparted the big secret that you'd started your period."

"Tell you about what?"

"Whatever it is that took the gilt off getting published. Whatever it is that has your chin dragging. Whatever it is that has your eyes rimmed with dark circles."

"I didn't know I looked that bad."

"Like Count Dracula's mother after the blood bank ran dry. What's the matter with you? This is supposed to be a celebration."

Elizabeth told Lilah about her lunch with Adam Cavanaugh and his notion to have a Fantasy in the lobby of each of his hotels.

"That sounds terrific, Lizzie! What's the problem? Other than the fact that you'd have to deal with *him*."

"The problems are too many to list, Lilah. I can't pack a suitcase and go city-hopping at the drop of a hat. I've got too many responsibilities here."

"Your kids would probably be better off if you left them now and then."

"And what about the money? I don't know anything about high finance. Do you realize the investment I'd have to make?"

"You said Cavanaugh offered to make you a business loan. Don't think of the investment, think of the profits," Lilah said, her eyes twinkling. "I'm surprised you're not grabbing this opportunity with both hands."

Elizabeth rubbed her forehead. The aspirin hadn't helped much. "I don't know, Lilah."

Lilah took Elizabeth's hand and lowered it to the table. "Does your indecision have anything to do with a certain neighbor of yours?"

Elizabeth's eyes swung up to her sister's. "I don't know what you're talking about."

"Lizzie," Lilah said, her tone softly reproachful,

"the kids told me about Matt's accident. The fruit bowl. The 'papers of Mom's that flew everywhere.' "

"Oh."

"They also said you got 'real mad' that Thad had read them." Lilah softened her voice even more. "Now even I have enough imagination to figure out what was on those pages that he read. One of your fantasies, right?"

"Right," Elizabeth said dismally.

"And you were embarrassed."

"Mortified."

"So you're avoiding him."

"Like the plague. I can't face him, Lilah."

"Just because he read one of your fantasies? That's ridiculous." Lilah saw the guilt spread over her sister's face like indelible ink. Elizabeth never could hide her feelings. "Uh-oh, *not* just because he read one. He read one and *applied* it to real life. Is that it?"

"Well, sort of," Elizabeth confessed.

"Lucky you."

Elizabeth was flabbergasted. "Lucky? Lilah, I was humiliated."

Lilah's eyes rounded and she whispered, "He's into *bondage*?"

"Oh, for crying out loud. No! He's not into— Can't you understand? He acted out my fantasy because he thought that's what I wanted."

"I'm dying to know all the salacious details, of course, but I realize you wouldn't tell me in a million years, even if we went back to summer camp. All I can say is that if I ever fall in love—and yes, I think you're in love with him—I'll buy all the sex manuals that are on the market.

"I'll underline all the good parts and earmark the illustrations that appeal to me and pass them to this fictitious guy and say, 'Hey, Charlie, I'm too shy to discuss with you my most secret desires, but I'd welcome you doing to me anything on these marked pages.' If Thad put to good use his knowledge of your heart and mind and libido, I would say he's worth his weight in gold. And if this is any consolation, I've never seen a guy more smitten."

Elizabeth looked up, begging to be convinced. "How do you know?"

"Easy. He stank to high heaven with jealousy of Cavanaugh. It was obvious to me and I don't even know the guy. Look," she said, standing up, "I'm gonna run upstairs and check on the kids. You sit here and think about what you really want to do with the rest of your life. Cavanaugh's proposal sounds like a dream come true, a real fantasy. On the other hand, Mr. Randolph is pretty fantastic himself. And he's closer to home."

Elizabeth sat alone at her kitchen table and asked herself what she wanted. If she could have her choice of anything at that very minute, what would it be?

The answer was unqualified. She wanted Thad.

She'd been more embarrassed than angry to discover he'd read her fantasy. She could admit that now. And she really hadn't suspected him of combing through her garbage can looking for discarded pages of manuscript. He was too straightforward to do something like that. Sure, he'd read that one fantasy on the sly, but as he'd pointed out, it was easy for him to do. After spotting several key words, no one could have resisted the temptation.

Yes, he had turned his knowledge to his advantage, but was that so bad? Lilah didn't think so. She thought he was a treasure for having put it to good use.

Come to think of it, how many men would care

enough about a woman to cater to her fantasies? Men that sensitive were rare, while those who held a degree in slam-bam-thank-you-ma'am were legion. He'd held back, patiently waiting for her to climax before letting himself. And hadn't he actually enjoyed the wait? She should have thanked him for being such a considerate lover. Instead she had slapped his face.

On her way upstairs, she met Lilah and the children trooping down. "We're ready, but you're headed in the wrong direction."

Breathlessly Elizabeth said, "Lilah, would you mind too terribly much if I skipped dinner with you tonight?"

"Aw, Mom."

"We want to go with Aunt Lilah. She asked us to—"

"You can go," Elizabeth hastily reassured her children. "If Aunt Lilah doesn't mind taking you by herself."

"Not if it's for a very good cause." Analytically, Lilah peered into her sister's eyes. They were several watts brighter than they'd been fifteen minutes earlier.

"It is."

Lilah grinned. "No, I don't mind taking them out alone. Come on, kids." They raced past her and out the front door, afraid that plans might be changed again.

"Lilah, I don't think I'll be writing any more fantasies, so please don't ask me to."

"Why not?"

"They're self-indulgent and self-centered. It's time I stopped dreaming about someone making love to me, and . . . and made love to some*one*. There's a big difference, you know."

"No, I don't. But I know you believe that."

"Someday, you'll know it too."

Lilah looked doubtful, then smiled softly. "Be happy with him, Lizzie. You deserve it." She lifted up the overnight bags she was holding. "I'm an optimist. I invited the kids to spend the night with me and they're already packed." Then, laughing all the way, she followed the children out.

Elizabeth waited until the front door clicked shut, then ran for the bathroom and reached for the taps in the tub. While it was filling with water and making a mountain of bubbles out of the scented gel she'd squeezed into it, she opened her closet and gave the contents careful consideration.

Twenty minutes later, she was ready. On her way through the kitchen, she took Lilah's bottle of champagne out of the fridge and left by the back door.

He was watching television on his enclosed porch. She knocked and saw his expression of glad surprise. He carefully masked that momentary reaction and, with an annoying lack of speed, came ambling toward the door. Unlike that other time, he rudely left the television volume up. He pushed open the door, but said nothing.

"May I come in?" she asked. He stepped aside. The porch was warm. The air smelled like him, like the wool sweater he was wearing over his jeans, like his cologne. Facing him, she moistened her lips.

"I'm sorry I slapped you. I was tremendously provoked or I never could have done such a thing." She paused to draw a tremulous breath. Unlike her sister, she wasn't impulsive. Didn't know how to be. What if this didn't work?

"I . . . I've thought about it for several days now and have realized that my accusations were ridiculous. I know you didn't sift through my garbage or anything like—"

"Elizabeth, what are you doing here?" he interrupted coldly. "Have you had a change of heart? Do you want me to fulfill another of your fantasies?"

She deserved that, she supposed. So she let him get by with it. This time. Instead of taking umbrage, she lifted her eyes to his. Her smile was as seductive as her whisper.

"No, I want to fulfill yours."

Ten

"And I always thought you were such a nice girl."

Elizabeth suspended nibbling on his bicep long enough to give him a feline smile. "I proved you wrong, didn't I?"

Replete, Thad sighed. "And then some."

She laid her head on his shoulder. "Actually, it took every ounce of courage I could muster to cross our backyards wearing nothing but high heels and a trenchcoat and my pride on my sleeve. I think I've been saving all my bravery from the day I was born for today."

Laughter rumbled out of his bare chest, which she was idly caressing with her fingertips. "I felt like I'd been hit by a two-by-four when you untied the belt of your coat."

"To say you were stupefied would be putting it mildly."

He turned his head and gazed down at her. "I wasn't sure you were real."

"I am."

He rolled over and pinned her beneath him. "How

well I know. Now." He kissed her thoroughly, and it was gratifying to learn that they weren't nearly as spent as they had thought they were. Already his manhood was firm with reawakened desire and the purring sound she made in her throat was most encouraging.

"My heart almost stopped when you reached for my fly and unzipped it," he whispered hoarsely. "And where'd you learn that trick with the champagne?"

"I made it up."

"You certainly did," he snarled.

She laughed at his double entendre. "I told you I wanted to indulge your fantasies."

"You exceeded them." He cupped her breasts in his hands and kissed them in turn. "You looked so pretty in the teddy."

"Then why didn't you let me wear it longer?"

"Because the best part was watching you take it off."

"Watching *us* take it off."

"You looked like you could use some help with those snaps." He nuzzled her neck.

Groaning, she dodged his ardent kiss, knowing that before they made love again, there were things that must be said. "Thad?"

"Hmm?"

"You are going to marry me, aren't you?"

He raised his head and looked down into her worried face. "I'm not sure. How good a cook are you?" She pinched his buttocks and he yelped. "Ouch! Okay, okay, I'll marry you." Then he laughed and hugged her tight. "Damn right I'm going to marry you. Knowing how your imagination works, do you think I'd let you run loose among the male population? Especially with FANTA C on the back of your car."

"I could never have done what I did this evening, I wouldn't be here at all, if I wasn't desperately in love with you." The seriousness with which she spoke sobered him.

"Know what?" He stroked her cheek tenderly. "If you hadn't taken the initiative, I would have. I'd have buried my anger, swallowed my pride, and come to get you. I wanted you that badly. And not just in my bed. Though you look damn good in it." His eyes ranged down her smooth nakedness, which was a perfect complement to his. "I need you in my life, Elizabeth."

"Matt and Megan?"

"The whole package."

"You're not used to their racket. You don't know how frustrating—"

He shushed her. "I'll learn to be a parent. I want to learn to be a good one. Now shut up and let me tell you how much I love you."

She acquiesced and fell silent. He ran his fingers through her hair. "I love you, Elizabeth. Admittedly it was lust at first sight. I wanted to make love to you at least a thousand times before I even thought of stopping."

His masculine smile curled her toes. "Then I got to know you and realized what kind of woman you are. Oh, I still want to be inside your body every chance I get. But I also want to be inside your head and inside your heart. I was a cynic who didn't believe there was such a thing as romance. There is. My head has been in the clouds ever since that day you got stuck in the tree and I had the honor of unsnagging your petticoat."

"I knew all about romance in my fantasies." Lovingly, she touched his lips. "But I didn't expect to find it in my own backyard. I don't need to expand my business to find a new challenge. Every day of loving you will—"

"Hey, whoa, back up. What was that about expanding your business?"

"Nothing. It doesn't matter now. Adam invited me to lunch today and made me an offer."

"What kind of offer?"

"Thad, I told you, it doesn't matter now. I'm going to marry you."

"What kind of offer?" he repeated stubbornly.

Sketchily she outlined the proposal Adam had made her. "But, of course, I'll have to turn him down now."

"Why?"

She gazed at him in amazement and gave a short laugh. "Why? Because I can hardly be a wife and mother and manage a chain of Fantasy stores all at the same time."

He propped his head on his hand. "Why not? I'll be a husband and father and manage my business all at the same time. If I have a career, why can't you? If you want one, that is."

She started to speak several times, but the words were tumbling through her head so rapidly she couldn't form a coherent sentence. Finally, smiling timidly, she said, "It would be a golden opportunity, the likes of which don't come along every day."

"Then go for it." He kissed her soundly. "You have my blessing."

"I'll give it some more thought, but I must say, the idea is sounding more tantalizing all the time." She twirled a clump of chest hair around her finger and glanced up at him from beneath lowered lashes. "What about Adam? I'd be spending a lot of time with him. Aren't you jealous of him anymore?"

"Nope. It wasn't his lap you were straddling a

while ago. And it wasn't his tongue licking champagne off your nipples. And your soft, warm mouth wasn't closed around—"

She laid her open palm across his lips. "Enough said."

He grinned. "Besides, I can't be too mad at him. The guy made me a fortune." Inquisitively, she angled her head to one side. "Every inch of concrete in the Hotel Cavanaugh was poured by Randolph Concrete Company. Didn't you know that?" She shook her head. "I doubt Cavanaugh realizes it, either, since I worked through the primary contractor. But in answer to your original question, no, I'm no longer jealous of him. I can't blame Cavanaugh for being attracted to you."

She turned rosy all over with pleasure. "It was never a sexual attraction between us. He likes me. I like him. But I could never love a man like him. He's too single-minded. Too driven by ambition. Too intense."

Thad rolled to his back and stacked his hands beneath his head. "What kind of man could you love?"

His conceit and complacency were endearing. She climbed over him, stretching her body lengthwise along his. She had the pleasure of watching his eyes turn hot with passion. "One just like you." She kissed his lips softly and murmured against them, "The one who stepped out of my fantasies."

THE EDITOR'S CORNER

I AM DELIGHTED TO WELCOME KATE HARTSON AS YOUR AUTHOR OF THIS MONTH'S EDITOR'S CORNER, AND TO LET YOU KNOW THAT NORA ROBERTS'S NEXT SIZZLING ROMANTIC SUSPENSE NOVEL—**SACRED SINS**—WILL COME OUT NEXT MONTH.

HAPPY HOLIDAYS!

Carolyn Nichols

I'm delighted to have joined the LOVESWEPT team as Senior Editor to work on these fabulous romances, and I'm glad to be writing the Editor's Corner this month so that I can say *hi* to all of you.

Isn't it a treat having six LOVESWEPT books every month? We never have to be without a LOVESWEPT in the bedroom, den, or purse. And now there are enough of these luscious stories to last through the month!

Soon we'll be rushing into the holiday season, full of sharing and good cheer. We have some special LOVESWEPT books to share—our holiday gifts to you!

RAINBOW RYDER, LOVESWEPT #222, by Linda Hampton, is a gift of excitement, as our respectable heroine, Kathryn Elizabeth Asbury, a pillar of the community, finds herself attracted to Ryder Malone, a wildly handsome rogue who has a penchant for riding motorcycles. Kathryn's orderly life is shaken by Ryder, who isn't quite what he appears to be. She fights hard for control
(continued)

but really can't resist this wild and free-spirited "King of the Road." Then she makes a thrilling discovery—and falling hard doesn't hurt a bit. **RAINBOW RYDER** is sure to be one of your favorites, but don't stop reading, we have five more LOVESWEPT GIFTS for you. . . .

Diamonds are the gift in Glenna McReynolds's **THIEVES IN THE NIGHT,** LOVESWEPT #223—how appropriate for the holiday season! Our heroine, Chantal Cochard, is an ex-jewel thief forced out of retirement when her family's prize diamond necklace shows up around some other woman's neck. DIAMONDS may be a girl's best friend, but they're not her lover. That's better left to well-built, sexy men like our hero, Jaz Peterson. Once Chantal invites him into her Aspen hideaway, she quickly learns that love is the most precious jewel of all!

Witty Linda Cajio's gift to us is **DOUBLE DEALING,** LOVESWEPT #224, a story of childhood dreams and adult surrender. Our heroine, Rae Varkely, mistress of a fabulous estate, is forced into a position where she simply has to kidnap Jed Waters. She makes a ransom demand, but our hero refuses to be released! Making demands of his own, he turns the tables on Rae, who can't help but pay with her heart. Still she has to protect her property from Jed's plans for development. But Jed has no intention of destroying anything—he only wants to build a strong relationship with the mistress of the manor.

A new book from Kay Hooper is always a gift, but **ZACH'S LAW,** LOVESWEPT #225, is an especially wonderful one. As the tale continues of those incredible men who work for Joshua Logan (and who indirectly fall out of SERENA'S WEB), we meet petite Teddy Tyler stranded on a deserted mountain road. Zach Steele, a strong, silent type who frightens Teddy because he ignites such strong desire in her, is her rescuer . . . then her sweet jailer . . . and the captive of her love. But Hagen's got his claws into Zach, there's mayhem on the horizon, and there's Zach's own past to confront before true love can win out!

(continued)

Sara Orwig's **OUT OF A MIST**, LOVESWEPT #226, is a gift of desire, as Millie and Ken are reunited after a brief but unforgettable encounter. Ken is on the run from the law, and Millie discovers him wounded and hiding in her closet. Of course, she knows he's done nothing wrong and she lets him stay with her until they can clear his name. But the longer he stays, the more he finds a place in her heart. Millie blossoms in Ken's embrace, but Ken won't settle for just passion—his desire is the lasting kind!

Our final romantic gift for you is a wonderful new book by Patt Buchiester called **TWO ROADS,** LOVESWEPT #227. This moving book is a story of healing: Nicole Piccolo is recovering from a broken leg and a broken heart, trying to forget Clay Masters, the man who promised her *forever* and then disappeared from her life. When Clay reappears a year later, the wounds are opened again, but Clay is determined to show Nicole that he never meant to leave and his heart has always been hers. When the healing is complete, they begin again with no pain to mar the exquisite pleasure of being in love.

Enjoy our gifts to you, sent with love and good cheer from your LOVESWEPT authors and editors!

Kate Hartson

Kate Hartson
 Editor
LOVESWEPT
Bantam Books, Inc.
666 Fifth Avenue
New York, NY 10103